HEARTS ON FIRE

EMILY HAYES

1

SCOTTI

The familiar sound of the wailing siren had Firefighter Scotti Saunders jumping to her feet automatically. Her body was moving before her mind caught up with her, but she didn't fight it. She had been in this job long enough to learn to trust her muscle memory and instincts.

Max called everyone to attention. "Alright, people, this is a big one—huge fire at a medical research facility downtown. There are a lot of doctors trapped in a section beyond the fire. We're obviously going there to save lives, but also as much of the equipment and computers as possible."

It went without saying that the trapped civilians came first. Scotti felt the usual curl of excitement in her belly as she followed the rest of her crew and quickly and smoothly started getting suited up. She loved her job, and big fires like this were particularly exciting.

Scotti got into the fire truck alongside Jeanette and Charlie, taking her usual place.

While Luke drove them toward the scene of the fire, Max gave them quick instructions.

"The facility has two entrances. We're lucky that it's lunch time, and a lot of the doctors are apparently together in the cafeteria. The team from Station 18 will go will go to the cafeteria through the front entrance, and you guys will go through the back and start searching and clearing offices and labs."

They pulled up at the huge building, which already sported flames leaping up to the sky and a lot of thick smoke. Scotti saw the fire truck from Station 18 arriving at the same time as they did. Scotti had smelt the smoke on approach. The smell of it always excited her. This was a big job, she could feel it and thrills ran through her body. Max quickly divided them into pairs, putting Scotti set to go through the back entrance to the offices and labs.

Her breathing apparatus was on her back before she exited the truck and she had twisted the cap to the tank of compressed air she would carry with her so she could breathe in the smoke filled building. As she descended from the truck she, she pulled on her mask, tightening it and taking a first big breath to get the air going. Scotti was so smooth with the motions, she had done it so many million times before. She pulled up her fire hood and put her helmet on. She was ready to go. She had her colleague next to her- they went everywhere in pairs for their own safety. She could see no signs of fire in this part of the building so she nodded to her colleagues and kicked the door in. Scotti knew that her colleagues were following her in, but she was now focused on the scene in front of her.

There were two corridors. Scotti gestured for Charlie to join her and they pulled one hosereel with them, while Jeanette and Luke took the other one.

As they progressed they checked and cleared off some smaller offices, more smoke was apparent the further they went into the building.

They came to a large lab, which was filled with smoke from some fire in the far corner.

"Fire department, call out!"

A weak cry answered Charlie's call and he hurried over. There were two doctors in white lab coats, who seemed disorientated and coughing with the smoke.

Scotti was about to help get them to safety when a soft cry reached her ears.

Charlie turned in the same direction as her. They were both primed to hear such cries for help, and to react to them.

"Go, I'll get these two out."

It wasn't necessarily protocol for them to split up. But Scotti and Charlie both knew when there were lives at risk, they would do what had to be done.

Scotti watched for a moment as Charlie pulled both of the doctors to their feet. They seemed mobile enough. He should be able to get them out of the building by himself.

Scotti kicked some debris aside to get to the door on the other side of the lab where she heard the call. It was clear to her the fire was the other side of that door along with the cries of somebody trapped.

Smoke seeped through the cracks around the door frame. Scotti had her hose reel ready and as she opened the door she sent some water in immediately.

She still staggered back a foot as she opened the door. The flames were spreading rapidly, the room was beginning to be overtaken by them. If there was someone in here, they wouldn't have much time.

Scotti loved her fire suit. She loved how it made her invincible to most fires. Obviously there were limits, but she loved how protected she was by it.

"Fire department, call out!"

"Here!" The voice was a bit louder now that Scotti was in the room, though still muted by the sound of the fire.

Scotti took a few steps closer, edging around the worst of the flames.

She winced as she finally made it through enough of the smoke to see clearly.

There was a doctor lying on the floor, a large beam pinning her down. It was clear that the fire had been above this room and the floor had started to collapse. Scotti would have to work quickly before the situation that was already bad got a whole lot worse.

She grabbed one end of the beam and tried to heave it off the doctor, but it was too heavy. Scotti doubted even Max could have lifted this by himself.

She grabbed her radio. “Charlie, I need assistance. Can you make it back to me? I’m in the room beyond the lab you left me in. One trapped casualty. The room is well on fire.”

Charlie took a second to respond. “Main corridor has caved in, I’ll have to find another way around. It may take me a few minutes.”

Crap. Scotti didn’t have a few minutes. “Come when you can,” she said shortly before cutting the radio. Charlie would make it here when he made it here. For now, she needed to work with what she had.

Scotti looked around and grabbed one of the freestanding desks and pulled it over to the beam. If she could use the desk as a lever, she might be able to lift the beam enough for the doctor to roll out.

She knew she had to move fast.

“Hey. Can you hear me?” She crouched down in front of the doctor, who looked only partially conscious. It was hard to see much at all in the smoke. The woman moaned and turned her head toward the sound of Scotti's voice.

"Wake up. Come on." Scotti shook her gently, casting an anxious glance at the advancing flames. She didn't have much time, but she had to keep a cool head or she could get them both killed.

The woman's eyes fluttered open.

"What's your name?"

"Naomi," she mumbled. Scotti couldn't see so clearly through the smoke but she could see wide frightened eyes that she knew she wouldn't forget.

"Naomi, it is ok. I've got you." She squeezed Naomi's hand through her thick fire glove. Something about this doctor clutched at Scott's heart. She knew she had to save her. "Naomi, you're going to have to help me. I'm going to lift the beam. When I do, I'm going to need you to roll to your left, out from under it. Can you do that for me?"

Naomi nodded. She blinked a few times, clearly trying to keep herself in the present moment.

Scotti hoped that Naomi could remain with it for long enough to help in her own escape, or they were both going to be in trouble.

She jammed the edge of the desk under the beam and pushed the other end down.

Scotti groaned as she put all her muscle into it. The side of the beam that was lying over Naomi slowly started to lift.

"Now, Naomi!"

Naomi rolled, flopping to the side of the beam. Scotti let it down carefully, not wanting to send debris flying if she dropped it. Unfortunately, the beam slipped at just the wrong moment, whacking her hard on the shoulder.

"Ow!" Scotti moved her shoulder gingerly, but it didn't seem broken. It felt sore, but at least it was still functional.

She hurried over to Naomi and turned her over. Naomi was barely with it, but at least she was no free from the beam. Now to get her out of there.

Scotti turned to the door she had came through but found it to be an impassable wall of flames. Well, that was just great. The room around her was burning and they didn't have long. She knew it was risky but she took her helmet off and started sharing her mask with Naomi so she took a couple of breaths and then switched back.

She scanned the room, looking for another way out. One of the walls to her left was collapsing under the pressure of the ceiling, which seemed to be caving in. It didn't look like a good way to get out.

Fuck.

Scotti looked around again but didn't see any way out of the room. She fought the familiar feeling of panic rising inside her. This was part of the job. She had to keep a cool head or she and Naomi were both dead.

"Charlie, I've freed the doctor, but we're trapped in here. How close are you?"

"I'm almost there, Scotti. I'm working towards you from the west side. Hold on."

"Got it."

Scotti grabbed Naomi and quickly pulled her away from the wall, moving them to the safest part of the room. She shielded Naomi with her own body and picked up her hosereel and began to put some water on the part of the fire where she was expecting Charlie to appear from.

Less than a minute later, the locked door to the west corridor imploded inward, revealing Charlie amidst a cloud of smoke and dust.

Scotti felt a smile sweep over her face.

"Man, am I glad to see you, Charlie."

Charlie went to work flooding the flames with water.

"Likewise. Let's get out of here. Max is calling us to pull out. This place is ready to collapse."

"Naomi, help me here, can you get over my shoulder. Not that one, this one. Don't worry, I've got you." Scotti pulled the jacket of her fire suit off and leant forward and the doctor who luckily was quite light was boosted by Charlie onto her good shoulder. Charlie put Scotti's fire jacket over the doctor as best they could to protect her.

"Let's go." Scotti said.

Scotti and Charlie started to head out of the building with the hose reel fighting flames as they came across them, with Naomi still holding on over Scotti's shoulder. An ambulance crew was already there awaiting them when they stumbled out of the building.

Scotti gingerly lifted the doctor to the ground aware of the pain in her shoulder. Naomi was still conscious, but barely and the ambulance crew immediately had an oxygen mask on her as they began to check her over. Her frightened eyes searched for Scotti again and Scotti met her gaze.

"Thank you," she murmured, her voice raspy from the smoke.

Scotti smiled at her. "It was nothing. Just doing my job," she replied, knowing that whenever there was a big fire, Scotti was always the one to go over and above what was required of her job. Scotti was known for taking risks and saving lives. She never thought twice about rushing into situations she might have been wiser to avoid.

She handed over to the waiting paramedics and went to join her team.

Max watched her suspiciously. "Firefighter Saunders! What happened to your arm?"

Scotti couldn't quite meet his eye. "Nothing."

"You're favoring your left. I *know* you always carry with your right."

"My arm is fine."

"Your shoulder?"

Fuck, he knew her too well.

"Some debris fell on it. I'm sure it's just bruised."

"Ambulance."

"Max! Honestly, it's not that bad."

"Ambulance, Scotti, now. Don't be difficult, now."

"I hate hospitals," Scotti grumbled, but she knew it was no use arguing with Max. She reluctantly got into a free ambulance.

"I'm fine," she told the paramedics. "My

shoulder is just bruised, and my captain is a worry-wart."

"We'll let the doctors decide that, ma'am."

"Yeah, yeah."

The ride to the hospital was short and Scotti was taken to the packed ER. Since her case wasn't urgent, she was in for a long wait.

She noticed the thick blonde pony tail coming towards her. Dr. Cora Hope. Scotti was familiar with the ER staff, both from her own visits and from delivering injured patients or colleagues.

"Hi, Dr. Hope."

"Oh, Scotti... I'm not happy to see you in my ER again."

Scotti shrugged, and then winced when it hurt her shoulder. "What can I say? I love it here. I missed you! How is your little girl?"

"Florence? Oh she is doing so well, thanks Scotti. She starts pre-school soon!"

"Wow, they grow up so fast. It only seems like yesterday that you were pregnant."

"I know! I can't believe it. We have been so lucky. She is just incredible, every day."

"She sure is lucky having two amazing moms like you and Dr. Frame."

Dr. Hope chuckled. "I'll have a good look at

your shoulder once things calm down here. For now, do you need anything for pain?"

"No, I'm okay. It doesn't hurt that much." If she didn't move it. Scotti kept that last piece of information to herself.

"Alright. Shout if you change your mind on the painkillers. I'll see you in a bit."

"Did you see the patient that I pulled from the fire? Naomi, her name is. How is she?"

Scotti didn't usually get invested in the people she saved after they were handed over to the ambulance—that was a recipe for heartbreak in this job—but she had felt something for Naomi. Something in her frightened eyes had touched Scotti in a way she hadn't been before.

"Dr. Naomi Crane? I hear it was a daring rescue!"

"You know me, always daring. Always rescuing."

Cora laughed. "Oh, I know. Always sweeping women off their feet!"

"Oh, you know me! So, how is she? This Dr. Naomi Crane? Will she be ok?"

"She's kind of a big deal in the medical world, Scotti. You really have probably saved millions of lives by saving hers."

"So, how is she?" Scotti felt determined to find out.

"Scotti, you know the drill. No giving out patient information to anyone except family."

Scotti could tell Dr. Hope knew how Naomi was.

"So ask her family."

Scotti knew from experience that families seldom had any problem with the firefighter who saved their loved one knowing the medical status of that loved one.

"She doesn't have any."

Scotti frowned. "Then who is going to advocate for her if she needs someone? If she's too ill to make her own decisions?"

There was almost always someone. Who didn't have any family?

"Oh, I don't think she will be needing someone to make her decisions."

That was a relief. Dr. Hope may not be allowed to tell Scotti Naomi's status, but if she didn't think that she'd need a step-in next of kin, then it couldn't be too serious.

"I'd better get going."

"Sure. Go do your job. I'll see you later."

A few minutes after Dr. Hope left, one of the nurses came over to check on her.

"No, Megs, I don't need any painkillers."

"Yeah, I figured. You are the big tough hero fire-fighter, Scotti Saunders. You would never admit to feeling pain. Also, you have a little cut above your eye that needs cleaning up. Anyway, it's not about that. Dr. Naomi Crane- I don't know if you know but she is a pretty famous doctor. Anyway, Dr. Crane is requesting to see the firefighter who saved her life."

Scotti felt her heart jump a little inside her. Apart from the thrill of a fire, Scotti always enjoyed the plaudits that came for the lives she saved.

Famous doctor, eh? Scotti vaguely recognized the name. She felt momentarily proud of herself for saving someone who was clearly a big deal. She remembered the brief connection she had felt with the doctor in the fire. When the heat and the smoke was closing in on them. When she had handed her own mask to the doctor so she could breathe clean air. When she had swung the doctor over her shoulder and felt her hands gripping tightly onto Scotti.

Scotti was suddenly aware of how filthy she was, covered in sweat, dust and grit and no doubt stinking of smoke, but she was pretty immune to that scent. She should likely have taken a shower, but it was too late for that now.

"Am I allowed to escape my bed, nurse?" Scotti was flirtatious as she always was. She couldn't help it. Anyone who knew her knew she was just playing.

"Only if you let me put your arm in a sling first."

Scotti rolled her eyes but nodded. Once Megs had attached the stupid sling, Scotti followed her to one of the many ER beds, this one cordoned off with curtains for privacy.

"Dr. Crane? This is Scotti Saunders, the firefighter who got you out."

Dr. Naomi Crane was sitting up in bed wearing an oxygen mask. Her hair was a mess and she was as filthy as Scotti, but that did little to detract from her beauty. During everything they went through, Scotti hadn't really had a chance to see properly or pay attention to how Naomi looked, but she certainly did now.

Naomi's bright green eyes shone through her soot-covered face and wild dark hair. She had high cheekbones and a perfect nose. She must have been mid to late 40s maybe, Scotti found it hard to be sure, there was a knowing wisdom in her eyes that came with experience of life.

There was little to see of her body through her shapeless hospital gown, but the swell of her breasts was enticing and made Scotti long to see more.

She forced her eyes up to Dr. Crane's face. She didn't want to be creepy. Dr. Crane obviously just wanted to thank her, not be ogled at by the lesbian firefighter.

Naomi pulled the mask off as she met Scotti's gaze, unflinchingly.

"Firefighter Scotti Saunders." She coughed. "Nice to properly meet you." She smiled weakly and her smile was dazzling. Scotti felt entranced by her. "And thank you for saving my life. I owe you a great debt of gratitude."

"Ah, it was nothing." Scotti smirked and raised her eyebrows. "Dead easy."

The doctor looked at her slightly perplexed and perhaps intrigued. Her lovely - but filthy- face was hard to read.

"I'm glad to see you sitting up, Dr. Crane. How are you doing?"

"Please. Call me Naomi."

"Naomi." Scotti said. "It is a beautiful name," she grinned at Naomi. "For a beautiful woman."

Flirting with big time doctors now, Scotti? Nice one.

"Thanks." Naomi seemed unphased by Scotti's charm and Scotti found her response- or lack of it- intriguing. Usually women either went to jelly around her, or their walls went up, or they just enjoyed laughing along with her flirting. Naomi had done none of these things.

"Minor smoke inhalation. They want to keep me overnight just in case, but they think I should be good to go tomorrow after some oxygen and observations."

It was as good as Scotti could have hoped for. "That's great. Smoke inhalation isn't fun, but one night isn't too bad."

"Not too bad, but I can't wait to get moved to a ward so I can get a shower. I don't know how you live like this, I'm filthy and all I can smell is smoke." Naomi seemed unimpressed.

"Well, I mean I certainly could do a shower too. So, just let me know if you want some company in there!" Scotti could see how dirty Naomi was and knew she would look just as much of a mess. She never usually cared about her post-fire look. It all just added to her own personal brand of firefighter charm.

"I never quite get rid of the smell of smoke from my hair, but usually women kind of grow to like the smell."

"I'm sure they do." Naomi again was hard to read and Scotti had no idea what the doctor was actually thinking.

"What about your arm? Broken?"

"No, fortunately not. I think my shoulder is just bruised. Nothing too serious, eh."

"Let me take a look." Naomi reached out her hand. Scotti immediately put her hands up in defence.

"Ah, I know you are some kind of big time doctor, but right now you are just a patient- don't worry about me."

"I'm always a doctor before anything else. I'm honestly doing fine. It's the least I can to take a look at your shoulder after you saved my life."

Scotti supposed it couldn't hurt to indulge her. She perched on the edge of Naomi's bed and gingerly removed the sling.

Naomi pulled Scotti's shirt back to examine her shoulder, which was already sporting a vivid bruise.

"Does it hurt when I do this?" She moved Scotti's arm gently.

"Yes." Scotti was trying not to be a baby, but it hurt a lot. She didn't want to look like a wimp in front of Naomi, though, so she did her best to keep her expression neutral.

"How about this?"

"Not as bad, but still sore. Ow! That one's a stabbing pain."

"I'm afraid it might be fractured, but you'll need an X-ray to be sure. I'll call Megs and have her take you up right away."

"I don't need to jump the line. I'm not an urgent case."

"I don't want to leave you waiting here for hours after the day you have had. Consider it a thank you favor for saving my life."

Scotti couldn't deny that the idea of leaving this place sooner rather than later was a good one. "Fine, but I don't want to be put above emergencies who really need the X-rays urgently."

"Of course not—Megs would never do that. You can, however, be put at the top of the waiting list for non-urgent cases."

"Thank you, I appreciate that."

"Thank *you*, Firefighter Saunders. I was so sure

I was going to die in there. I don't remember much —it only comes in flashes—but I remember your face and your voice and how you were so calm and found a way to keep me alive and get us out. You saved me, and I'll be forever grateful."

"Call me Scotti. For sure, call me Scotti."

Scotti felt herself blushing. "Anyway, it's just my job," she mumbled.

"Risking your own life to save mine makes you a hero, whether it is your job or not."

"You save lives as well, though. People tell me you are a hero doctor."

Now, it was Naomi who was almost blushing. "I do my best. I love what I do."

"Me too. People think I'm crazy for running into burning buildings, but it's what I live for. Only my fire colleagues really understand."

"I get that. I sometimes feel like my fellow doctors are the only ones who really understand me."

Scotti knew that she should leave Naomi to rest, but she was enjoying talking to Naomi too much to end it just yet. She was drawn to Naomi's clear intelligence and confident manner. She was even more than Scotti had imagined a top doctor would be, and Scotti felt borderline intoxicated by her presence. Clearly, she was more into intelligent older women than she had realized.

"Dr. Hope said that you didn't have any family here."

It wasn't a question, but Naomi answered it anyway.

"My parents are both dead, and my sister lives in the UK. She'd fly over if I asked her to, but given that this isn't anything overly serious, I told Megs not to contact her, not yet. I'll give her a call when I'm not coughing anymore."

"You'd best text her in the meantime. That fire is all over the news, and she'll probably be frantic when she finds out."

"That's a good point. Did you see my... oh, right. My phone was in the lab with me. It's probably a charred brick by now."

Scotti grimaced in sympathy. "Do you know her number by heart? You can borrow my phone."

"Thanks, Scotti, I'd appreciate that."

Scott handed over her phone and Naomi sent a quick text.

Megs poked her head through the curtains. "Scotti? They're ready for you at the X-ray department."

"Perfect. I'll check in on you later, Naomi."

It turned out that Scotti's shoulder was just bruised, much to her relief. She was dead on her feet, but refused the bed Dr. Hope offered her, insisting that she could take a cab home.

As soon as she got home, Scotti finally showered and felt real pleasure at finally feeling clean again. She lay down in bed. She texted in her work group that she had been discharged and was fine so that they wouldn't worry and fell asleep almost instantly.

The next morning, she was woken early by her alarm, as usual. Scotti grimaced as she got out of bed. Her shoulder had stiffened up overnight and she could barely move it.

As much as she hated the idea, she wasn't going to be able to work with it like this. She'd head over to the hospital to get something for it. Painkillers wouldn't do—she couldn't work with too many of those in her system either—but maybe they could give her an injection of something that would make it looser, at least enough for her to work.

Scotti hated being off work for injuries. She didn't have many hobbies outside of work, which left her at home with nothing to do but dwell on the inconvenience of whatever was keeping her away from her job.

Dr. Hope was on again, and since today was a quiet day, she was able to see Scotti immediately.

"Hey, Scotti. The shoulder bothering you?" Scotti liked Cora Hope. She was always kind and always smiling.

"Yeah. Can you give me something that'll allow me to work through it?"

She knew Dr. Hope wouldn't be keen.

"Scotti, you know the drill. You rest until injuries are healed, not push through them."

"It's just bruised! It's not like it's broken or even strained. It's not going to hurt to have it a little looser so that I can work, is it?"

"It'll feel even worse tomorrow if you do."

"But will it cause more harm?"

"No," Dr. Hope admitted, "but you'll feel like crap when the injection wears off. You'd have to come in every day for at least a week for repeats until the bruising has healed on its own."

"Fine, I'll do that, then."

Dr. Hope sighed. "Alright, but you need to tell your captain everything before you go to work. He'll make the call as to whether or not you can be on duty."

"Dr. Hope!" Scotti whined, "you know what he'll say."

"That's my condition, take it or leave it."

"Fine," Scotti grumbled, already fishing her phone out of her pocket. She dialed Max's number.

"Scotti. How are you feeling?"

"I'm fine. My shoulder is a bit stiff, but I'm ready to come back to work."

"That's great. Did you need anything in particular before you come in?"

Scotti grimaced. "I may... need an injection in my shoulder before I come in. Just to loosen it up a bit."

"No."

"Max! Dr. Hope says I'll be fine. Just sore. I can handle the pain."

"If your shoulder is bad enough that you need an injection for it, it's bad enough that you can't work. Take the injection, and if it's feeling significantly better tomorrow, you can come in. Today, I'm booking you off."

Scotti resisted the urge to argue. Arguing with Max would just get her booked off for even longer. "Fine. I'll see you tomorrow."

"Maybe. You'd better not lie about that

shoulder."

"I won't," Scotti sighed. She wasn't always the best about declaring injuries, but she wouldn't lie outright if asked, and Max was sure to ask.

She hung up and gave Dr. Hope a sour look. "He says I can't work today. I can come in tomorrow if the injection has helped my shoulder a lot."

"That sounds like a good decision. If we loosen it up today and you don't work it, it should be significantly better by tomorrow."

The injection stung, but Scotti didn't really mind, as long as it would get her back to work quickly.

"Is Dr. Crane still here?"

"You can check. I know she was being discharged this morning, but I'm not sure what time. Agnes checked in on her earlier and said she was doing really well."

Scotti wandered over to the general ward and asked at the nurses' station for Dr. Crane. She was in luck; Naomi was just packing up her stuff to go.

Scotti hurried to her room, wanting to catch her before she left.

Naomi looked good this morning. She had clearly showered and found a hair brush from somewhere and they had given her some clean scrubs to go home in. She looked squeaky clean, clear skinned and her hair was neatly brushed back in a low bun.

Scotti felt her heart leap. She looked beautiful.

"Good morning Dr. Crane. How are you doing today?"

Naomi looked up at her and smiled. "Fire-fighter Saunders! It's good to see you. I'm doing alright. One of my colleagues brought some scrubs and toiletries for me and I got a shower last night and again this morning, so things are looking up."

"That is a plus. Do you need a ride home?"

"That would be great, actually. I was just going to get a cab. Obviously, my car isn't here. What are you doing here, though? I didn't expect to see you again—not that I'm not happy you're here."

"I needed to get my shoulder checked again. Nothing to worry about."

Naomi raised an eyebrow. "Trying to sneak back to work before it's fully healed? I know your type."

"Guilty," Scotti laughed. "My captain put a stop to it, though. I'm hoping he'll allow me back tomorrow."

"Good for him. Pushing yourself too soon will only lead to further injury."

"I know, I know. I just don't like it."

"I get that. I hate being away from work, too."

Scotti took Naomi's bag and the two of them walked out of the hospital.

They were met by a wall of reporters.

"What the hell?" Scotti murmured.

"Oh no," Naomi groaned. "It must have gotten out that I was being discharged this morning."

"Um. I heard you were some kind of famous doc, but this is a *lot* of reporters."

Naomi turned and ushered Scotti back inside the hospital.

"Didn't you see it?"

"See what?"

"Come back inside, let me show you."

The nurses shooed the press away as Scotti and Naomi retreated into the relative peace of the hospital reception area.

"One of my colleagues showed me last night. Just google my name."

"Dr. Naomi Crane?" Scotti felt dumb as soon as she said it.

"That is my name." Naomi raised an eyebrow

and looked so damn attractive Scotti felt a rush of desire run through her.

Scotti picked up her phone and googled Naomi's name and was immediately bombarded by dozens of articles.

Hero firefighter saves celebrity doctor and many other headings like it were accompanied by a video.

Scotti opened it and was surprised to see herself rescuing Naomi from under that beam. It was an infrared camera feed so you couldn't see loads but you could see enough. She had to admit, it did look impressive, but she was too confused to pay much attention to the content of the video. It then followed up with footage of her carrying Naomi out of the building.

"How does this video even exist? CCTV?"

"The on-site security cameras submit a live feed to another location. Apparently, they were still working when you rescued me. Someone must have sold the footage to the press."

"You don't look particularly unhappy about it."

Naomi shrugged. "They didn't reveal any of the confidential work that was happening before the fire. I don't really care if someone sees you pulling me out of a burning building—unless you do? I'm sure we could get a court order to get it taken down..."

"No, that's alright; I don't care one way or the other. It's just a surprise. So that's why all the reporters are camping out on the hospital doorstep. Do we do anything about them?"

"Well, do you want to give an interview?"

"Um... no?"

"Then you don't have to," Naomi assured her. "They'll try to force you, but you still get to say no. You might want to check with Max—it would be good publicity for the station—but even if he wants you to, it's still your choice. I'll probably do an interview with them at some point, but right now, I just want to be at home."

"You must be used to dealing with the press, with your job and prestige."

Naomi shrugged. "I'm somewhat used to it, but I have to admit, I've never had a crowd quite that large after me."

Scotti glanced nervously at the door. "Can we even get past them? They look like they might attack if we refuse them."

Naomi laughed. "Don't worry, you'll be fine. Just stick close by me. I'll protect you. Where's your car?"

"On the other end of the lot," Scotti groaned. "Maybe we should get security to clear them."

"That won't look very good for the hospital, to have security clearing out reporters. Honestly, Scotti, you run into burning buildings for a living. You can handle a couple of reporters."

"That's more than a couple!"

"You can't fool me; I already know you're brave. Now enough procrastinating. Let's go."

Scotti allowed Naomi to lead her outside.

The reporters exploded into questions, shoving cameras and microphones into both of their faces.

"No comment at this time," Naomi said calmly. "I'll be giving an interview once I feel a bit better. For now, please leave us be."

Of course, the reporters did no such thing—not that Naomi had expected them to.

Naomi was maybe right, the rush of fighting through reporters wasn't dissimilar to that of fighting through burning buildings.

Once they got in the car and away, Scotti felt Naomi's hand touch her thigh. The bolt of desire ran through her again.

Who on earth was this doctor she had saved and what might happen between them?

2

NAOMI

They made it to Scotti's pick up, and Naomi gratefully slammed the door shut. Scotti had to hit the horn a few times to make the reporters move out of their way, but they finally gained the peace of the highway.

Naomi glanced at Scotti out of the corner of her eye as they drove. She hadn't missed how attractive Scotti was last night, and today, with Scotti freshly showered, it was even harder not to pay attention to.

Scotti had short blond hair and blue eyes. Her arms were well-muscled, and Naomi knew that Scotti had easily lifted her up with those arms. Naomi couldn't help but wonder what it would feel like to have Scotti lift her up onto a counter surface and kiss her until she was dizzy.

She wondered if Scotti would be open to the idea. Naomi knew Scotti had been flirting with her, there had been some fairly *interesting* chat up lines, but Naomi wasn't sure whether that was just how she was. Naomi had worked her way into a position in life where she was used to getting what she wanted, and right now, she wanted Scotti.

That was when she had put a hand on Scotti's thigh as she drove and she felt Scotti's muscles tense under her hand and her breathing quicken. That was when she knew for sure that Scotti was into her.

They arrived at Naomi's house and Scotti walked Naomi to the door. Fortunately, the reporters all seemed to have been at the hospital, and they made it to the door without having to fight their way there.

"Do you want to come in?" Naomi's question was loaded.

"Sure, that would be great." Scotti easily replied.

Naomi practically skipped inside, delighted that Scotti had accepted her offer. She didn't usually relate well to other people and was surprised by how at ease she felt with this fire-fighter when they were clearly so very different.

It was probably just because Scotti had saved her life—such bonds were quite natural to form under such extreme circumstances—but Naomi still enjoyed being able to feel like this with some-one. She admired Scotti's bravery and her clear compassion for the people she saved.

"What would you like to drink?"

"Whatever you're having will be fine."

"I don't know if firefighters drink wine, but I'm having wine."

Naomi got out one of her fancier bottles of wine and poured them each a glass. Scotti took a sip and murmured her appreciation.

"Oh, I'm easy. I'll drink anything. I needed this. Not being able to work sucks." Scotti's strong hands made the wine glass look small and deli-cate. Naomi couldn't help but imagine what else Scotti's strong hands could do.

Mmmm, those fingers.

"Yeah, I know the feeling. I've got a fairly robust immune system from working in a hospital, but every now and then, I catch something from a patient and can't go into surgery until I'm completely better. It drives me crazy."

"I see we share an addiction to our jobs. And perhaps an addiction to saving people." Scotti grinned. Her teeth were neat and white and her smile was charming. Scotti was so very handsome, some kind of beautiful blend of masculine with a feminine twist. "How long are you on time out for?" she asked.

"Well, given my research facility burned down, it would have been quite a while, but I'm trying to sort out something with the chief of surgery so that I can come back to the hospital earlier than I had originally planned when I took time away from surgery for research."

"Do you think that'll work?" Scotti looked up at her. Her eyes were dark blue under a floppy blonde fringe. Her face was tanned and heavily freckled across her nose.

Naomi wanted her in a way she hadn't wanted anyone in a long time. Naomi was quite sure that someone who looked like Scotti and with her effortless charm, probably had this affect on most women, but she didn't resist it.

"I think so. They can always use my help; it'll just take a bit of admin work to get it approved."

They chatted for a few minutes about work before the conversation turned to interests.

"No way. You own a *Ferrari?* Why aren't you driving it? That's practically criminal wastage!" Scotti's face was outraged.

"I can't drive it around as a normal car! It is anything but a normal car! I drive it on weekends or off days. I'll go for long drives out on the roads that no one uses where you can see for miles."

"Including cops," Scotti commented shrewdly.

Naomi shrugged. "You got me. What's the point in owning a car like that if you can't put its speed to the test?" Driving fast in her beautiful car was one vice that Naomi did enjoy.

"You have to show me!"

"Now?"

"Fuck, yeah."

Naomi put down her wine and got up, delighted that Scotti seemed to share her interest in cars. She led Scotti through to the garage and flicked on the light.

Scotti moaned softly as she saw the Ferrari, making Naomi wonder how her moans would sound in an entirely different context.

"Do you want to drive it?"

Scotti turned to her with wide eyes. "Can I?"

"I don't usually let other people behind the

wheel, but for someone who has just saved my life, I can make an exception."

Scotti hesitated. "I don't want you to think you owe me anything, Naomi. I was doing my job and I was glad to do it. You don't have to thank me."

"I may not have to, but I want to." Naomi took the keys down from the board hanging on the garage wall and tossed them to Scotti, who caught them by reflex.

"You're on. Direct me to your best route."

Naomi was more nervous than she let on. She loved this car and had never let anyone else drive it before, but Scotti's enthusiasm was infectious, and Naomi found that she loved seeing Scotti this excited.

She had to give credit where credit was due—Scotti was a good driver, and she was extremely careful with the car. Naomi directed Scotti to one of her favorite back roads—a long one seldom populated by other cars, let alone cops—and told her to go crazy.

Scotti slowly accelerated, gaining confidence as the car purred happily beneath her.

"Can I roll down the windows?"

"Of course. It's better that way."

As they accelerated further, the wind whipping

their hair around, Scotti laughed, a sound of pure joy, and Naomi found herself laughing along as well.

Naomi had driven the car to its limits many times before, but she found that she enjoyed being with Scotti while Scotti drove just as much.

"This is amazing! I never thought I'd get to drive one of these."

"I'm glad I could offer you the experience."

Scotti slowed down well before the road hit a turn, and Naomi gave directions to get back to her place. Naomi watched the sides of the garage carefully as Scotti backed the car in, but Scotti avoided them easily. She was an absolute natural driver. Naomi enjoyed the effortless way that Scotti handled the car and she let her mind wander imagining how Scotti would effortlessly handle her body.

Scotti was slightly flushed as she turned the car off. The garage lights were still on, providing enough illumination for Naomi to see her clearly.

Scotti turned to Naomi, beaming. "Come on a date with me."

"What?"

"Well, that was kind of the best first date ever,

but we never agreed it was a date, so... come on an official date with me?"

Naomi's feeling of ease and happiness stiffened. She didn't want to hurt Scotti's feelings, but she had to be honest. Her and Scotti's connection felt magnetic and intense and became more so with every minute they spent together. And she definitely wanted to have sex with Scotti. But...

"I can't."

Scotti's face fell. "Oh. Okay."

"Okay? Don't you want to know why?"

"Of course I do, but you don't owe me an explanation, Naomi. If you don't want to go on a date, you don't want to go on a date. If you want to share why, you will. If not, I'm not going to interrogate you about it."

Why did Scotti have to make saying no so damn hard? She really was perfect, wasn't she?

Despite what Scotti said, Naomi felt that she owed her an explanation. The question was, how did she explain it without offending Scotti?

"The last person I dated died," she blurted out.

"Oh, Naomi... I'm so sorry."

"We weren't serious. It was just a fling, really, but it still hit me pretty hard. She was a police officer and died in the line of duty. I can only imagine how bad it would have been for me if we were serious. After that, I swore I'd never date anyone in such a dangerous line of work again."

"So it's my work that's the problem."

"Please, Scotti, don't think I have a problem with what you do. On the contrary, I greatly admire you and your colleagues. Hell, I wouldn't be alive if there weren't people brave enough to do what you do. I'm simply saying that it makes us incompatible as a couple. However, if you're willing, I would like to be friends."

Scotti considered this for a moment. "I would like that. I think we'd make a great couple, but I respect your decision on that. With that option off the table, I do believe we can also be great friends."

Naomi let out a small breath of relief. "I think so too, Scotti."

But, I still want to have sex with her. So, what do I do about that?

3

SCOTTI

Scotti knew that this wasn't a date, but she felt more excited than she had been for any date before. When Naomi had said that she could get them tickets to a very exclusive car exhibition of some of the world's best cars, she'd jumped at the opportunity.

Apparently, Naomi had saved the daughter of the man who was running the exhibition, and he'd even promised her a test drive of a car of her choice. Naomi had negotiated a passenger for the test drive. Scotti was practically drooling at the thought.

Scotti dressed fancy, as per Naomi's instructions. She'd had to go to the store to get something suitable, as she'd never been to any fancy events before. Such events weren't usually Scotti's thing. This particular event, however, was a glaring exception to that rule.

Naomi was picking Scotti up, as they wouldn't let Scotti in alone. Naomi had arranged for Scotti to come with her, but apparently they were very strict on who they let in, and Scotti would need to be by Naomi's side to allow her entrance.

Scotti was hardly complaining. Any time spent alone in an enclosed space with Naomi was good with her. It might drive her crazy, shooting down thoughts of how good it would be to kiss Naomi and wondering how she would moan if Scotti reached just a little lower... but it was still worth it.

Naomi rang the bell and Scotti hurried to answer it. When she saw Naomi, her jaw dropped. Naomi was wearing a long black dress that hugged her hips and flared elegantly down at the bottom. Naomi's body looked incredible- even though Scotti had been having all these illicit thoughts about Naomi, she had actually never seen her in anything figure hugging. She enjoyed running her gaze over the beautiful curves of Naomi's breasts, hips and ass.

Her dark curls were piled and pinned on top of her head and her green eyes were sparkling.

Scotti noticed a tattoo on the back of her shoulder blades. She hadn't expected that. But then she hadn't expected the ferrari either.

It seemed Dr. Crane was full of surprises.

She immediately regretted her own choices—a bright red satin button down shirt with flames sewn around the collar. She had matched it with a black pant suit and she usually loved the attention she got in it. But today, she should have gone with something more classic. She wasn't going to fit in among all the other fancy people—

Naomi's voice interrupted Scotti's mental spiral. "Scotti... you look incredible! Did you get that custom made? It's perfect for you."

"Really? You think it's suitable?"

"Suitable? Every person there is going to be green with envy. It's perfect."

Scotti smiled in relief. "You know, you don't look too bad yourself."

"Please, I've seen myself in the mirror. Admit it, I look hot."

"You do," Scotti admitted. She knew she should keep it at that, but Naomi had started this conversation, hadn't she? "More than hot, really. You look truly incredible." Scotti was forthright in her honesty.

Naomi blushed a little. "Thanks."

Scotti followed her outside to find they were taking the Ferrari to the event. Riding in the Ferrari alone would have been enough motivation for Scotti to go pretty much anywhere.

She examined the exquisite interior as Naomi pulled out onto the street and started driving. She handled the car expertly, her expression relaxed as other cars passed nearby. Scotti, on the other hand, had to stop herself from biting her nails in worry that this beautiful car might be desecrated by a scratch or bump from a careless driver.

"Relax. I'm a good driver and I've got great insurance."

"You're right. I'm just being paranoid."

"Not really paranoid. There are a lot of bad drivers out there. But I'm not going to let them stop me from enjoying my car."

"That's a good attitude to have. It would be a shame to let a beauty like this go to waste."

"Exactly."

They arrived at the event venue, and Scotti saw why Naomi had decided on the Ferrari. They would surely look out of place in anything else.

Had Naomi not shared with her a list of the cars that would be at the exhibition, Scotti would have been content to remain in the parking lot and ogle at the fine specimens here.

Scotti was also relieved to find that her flame collared shirt wasn't out of place at all. There were plenty of people in classically cut black dresses and suits, but there were just as many in more colourful attire.

Naomi gave their names at the door, and they were admitted after being checked off a list. Scotti's breath caught in her throat as they stepped into the main room. Despite knowing what would be there, she still found herself caught off guard by the beauty and majesty before her.

"Naomi, look," Scotti breathed. She grabbed Naomi's hand without thinking about it and practically dragged her over to an Aston Martin—the Valkyrie, no less. Naomi didn't seem to mind at all. She was staring avidly at the car, with an expression of adoration that Scotti guessed must be similar to her own.

They walked around the car, admiring it from every angle before moving on. Naomi chose the next car to look at—an Aspark Owl. The design was unusual, but no less spectacular for it.

The two of them wandered between cars, barely paying attention to anyone else.

Scotti realized that they were still holding hands and made no move to change that situation.

She imagined kissing Naomi and bending her over one of these cars to fuck her from behind... and quickly stopped. Those thoughts were far too tempting, despite the many people around.

Scotti lost track of time as she and Naomi admired the cars, talking enthusiastically about the various pros and cons of each model.

"Scotti... we need to make a decision now about the car for the test drive. They're closing soon, so we need to get going or we're going to miss the opportunity."

"Oh! I didn't realize how quickly the time had passed. But it's your test drive—you should choose."

"I was thinking we could choose together."

Scotti's insides flared with pleasant warmth at the idea that Naomi would share this choice with her. "Well, it's a tough call, but for me it's the Bugatti Mistral."

"I was also leaning toward Bugatti, but the Bolide is the one that really does it for me."

This, of course, sparked another lively debate

between the various pros and cons of the two cars. Both Scotti and Naomi stood by their picks and agreed to flip a coin. Naomi won, something Scotti was secretly glad for—it was Naomi's test drive, after all. She should get to drive the car she wanted to drive.

Naomi had to sign a bunch of forms, but eventually, she and Scotti were allowed into the car. The engine came to life beneath them, a truly beautiful sound.

Scotti was practically vibrating with excitement. Naomi drove carefully through the city until they got to the same road she and Scotti had used the last time.

Then, she really floored it. She rolled the windows down and the two of them laughed in delight as they practically flew across the ground.

This was incredible. It didn't matter that Scotti wasn't the one driving. Seeing Naomi's face as she drove, lit up with joy even as her sharp eyes watched the road, was a treat in itself.

Scotti admired her capable hands on the steering wheel. She imagined those same hands in surgery saving lives. Her hands were graceful yet strong. Her nails were short and neat and immaculately clean.

Naomi came to a halt near the end of the road and pulled off to the side. She was breathing hard —they both were, Scotti realized.

"Why are we stopping here? I hope we're not planning to steal this car, because—"

Her words were cut off by Naomi's lips on hers. Scotti grabbed Naomi's ass to steady her—she had practically lunged across the center of the car to reach Scotti.

Scotti didn't need asking twice. She pulled Naomi into her lap—she must have taken her seat-belt off when they stopped—and kissed her with equal enthusiasm.

It only lasted a few moments, but those moments were as hot as any fire Scotti had ever gone into.

"No."

Scotti pulled back to look at Naomi, removing her hands from Naomi's waist. "No?"

"No, we can't do this."

Scotti frowned. "Then why did you kiss me?"

Naomi scrambled awkwardly back over to the driver's seat. "I'm sorry, Scotti. I… I lost control."

"Maybe that's not such a bad thing. I want you. It seems to me like you want me too. Let's give this a try. Worst that can happen is that we don't work out."

"No, it's not," Naomi said sharply. "The worst that can happen is that I fall wildly, passionately in love with you and then you *die.* That would break me."

"You can't go through your life assuming the worst, Naomi. That's no way to live."

"It's the way I choose to live my life, and it's a valid choice. Not everyone is brave like you, Scotti. I'm not going to risk my heart like that."

Scotti supposed that Naomi had a point, but she still didn't like that Naomi had kissed her knowing that she hadn't changed her mind. She didn't like being messed around with like that. She deserved better, and she had thought better of Naomi.

"I think we should go back."

"Scotti, please don't be upset. I'm sorry, okay? I shouldn't have kissed you. I promise, I won't do it again."

"Yeah, you won't. I think I'll get out here. I can take a taxi home."

"No, Scotti, wait—"

Scotti opened the door and got out. She walked

away and was both relieved and disappointed when Naomi didn't follow her.

She knew she was overreacting. She should just let Naomi drive her back, but she was hurt—hurt that Naomi would kiss her and not mean it, and hurt that Naomi would still reject her because of her career despite the obvious connection they shared.

Scotti walked a block away before sitting down on the sidewalk and calling a taxi.

She reflected sadly that as much as she wanted it, Naomi had to want it too. They simply weren't meant to be.

4

NAOMI

Naomi checked her phone again, but all she had was spam messages. Nothing from Scotti.

She didn't even know why she was still checking her phone. It had been three weeks. If Scotti was going to contact her, she would have done so by now. They had agreed to be friends, but Naomi had messed all that up with her moronic loss of self-control.

It seemed that Scotti had moved on from the brief but intense connection they had shared.

Naomi only wished that she could do the same.

She told herself it was for the best. She and Scotti barely knew each other, and Naomi's emotions were already spinning around, untethered and uncontrolled. This was the main reason she didn't do relationships. Women made her crazy. How could she focus on her research if she was being driven crazy by some hot muscly firefighter? She didn't know exactly what it was she felt for Scotti, but it was intense, twinged with both pleasure and fear—fear for what it could mean.

She couldn't develop feelings for a firefighter. That simply wasn't optional. Better to stay away before she could get in over her head. Why was it always these tough hero women she was into?

Naomi was about to go into her next surgery when her pager started beeping frantically.

She glanced at it and leaped out of her chair. She was sure that surgeons all over the hospital were doing the same. There was a multi-car pile-up not far from them and the rescue teams needed assistance in stabilizing patients.

Ambulances were already leaving the hospital. Naomi got into the nearest one alongside the paramedics and they sped off.

The scene of the accident was utter chaos. It was difficult not to trip over shrapnel due to the stinging smoke in the air. It looked like at least one of the cars was on fire. The firefighter who seemed to be in charge hurried over to Naomi.

"You're the cardio surgeon?"

"That's right."

"I'm Captain Roddis. You're needed over there —there's a man with a steel rod through his chest. We want to get him out, but we need your expertise, Ma'am."

Naomi wondered how the hell steel rods entered into this messed up equation, but she didn't want to take the time to ask.

She went in the direction Max was pointing and saw the bottom half of a firefighter poking out of a car. She saw now how steel rods had gotten involved—it looked like they had fallen off the back of the truck just in front of this car and pierced the windshield.

"Hi, I'm here to help. I'm Dr. Crane, a cardiothoracic surgeon."

The firefighter pulled her head out of the car, and Naomi was surprised to see the tousled blonde hair and intense dark blue eyes beneath the helmet. Of all the firefighters in the world. Of course it had to be Scotti. Of course, she shouldn't really be surprised; she and Scotti worked in the same city, and they were bound to run into each other on calls every now and then.

"Dr. Crane. Hi." Scotti stared at her for a moment before pulling herself back to the present moment. "I need your advice here. Take a look and tell me if it's safe to move him. I've cut the rod as close as I can to his chest, but it'll still be jostled as I get him out."

She moved back and Naomi took her place. The man was close to unconscious, his pulse thready and weak. He was losing a lot of blood, probably a slash from one of the steel rods.

"We can't move him yet. I need to get this other wound stitched up or he'll bleed out before he can make it to the hospital. Hand me my bag?"

Scotti held out the medical bag, and Naomi got to work. The wound had come perilously close to an artery, though thankfully it hadn't been severed. Naomi had her work cut out for her, working in such a cramped space with a limited selection of tools. Even once she had sorted this wound, she wasn't sure she rated the patient's chances given the location of the penetrating steel rod. It was hard to tell exactly what was going on inside.

"Here." Scotti was suddenly beside her, wiping the sweat off Naomi's face with a spare bandage.

Scotti's fingers brushed her skin and she liked the touch.

"Thanks." Naomi had her hands busy and she didn't think that sweat dripping into the patient's wound would be particularly helpful, so she was grateful for Scotti's intervention.

"Pass me more thread, please? It's in those little packets in the side of the medical bag."

Scotti handed over the thread and Naomi continued with her work of stitching the wound closed.

"Okay, there. He should be stable to transport now—but watch the end of that rod. If it catches on anything..."

"Don't worry, I'll be careful. Here, move out of the way so I can get in. Looks like I'll need to make the space a bit bigger if I'm going to get him out without causing any extra movement."

Naomi stepped back to let Scotti do her work. She watched as Scotti used a huge jaw-like machine to pry the sides of the car further open before crawling in. Even though she was in a bulky uniform, Naomi couldn't help staring.

Scotti was so hot like this, immersed in her job, her face set in concentration, her pants tightening over her ass as she leaned forward into the car.

Naomi knew it was completely inappropriate to be turned on right now, but Scotti wasn't helping matters. Did she have to be so damn attractive?

When the patient was pulled out of the car, Naomi thankfully forgot all about her inappropriate feelings as she focused on getting him to the ambulance. His pulse was stuttering worryingly, but the best thing for him was to get him to the hospital as soon as possible so he could get into surgery and they could get to work fixing him.

Scotti helped Naomi load him onto a stretcher and hand him over to the paramedics. As much as Naomi wanted to go with him and perform the surgery herself, she knew that she was needed here. There were doctors at the hospital who would be waiting to do the surgery when he arrived.

"Dr. Crane! This way, come on."

Scotti gestured Naomi over, distracting her from her contemplation of the retreating ambulance. She hurried after Scotti to a nearby car. They worked together to extract the two people in there, Scotti making room for Naomi to get in and stabilize the patients before pulling them out.

They went from car to car, working until the

first responders were the only ones left on the scene. Naomi sat heavily down on an empty stretcher, stretching her aching muscles. She was filthy and desperately needed a shower, but she was too tired to move just now.

"Naomi? Would you like to come back to the fire station and take a shower? Our station is just near here. It looks like all the ambulances are gone."

That was true. Naomi could call a taxi to take her home or back to the hospital, but it seemed silly when Scotti was offering her a quick route to what she wanted most—to wash off all the blood and grime. She was exhausted.

"Sure. That would be great, thanks."

Naomi and Scotti got into the fire truck, sitting down next to each other. The seats were close together and their knees were touching. Naomi glanced at Scotti, only to find that Scotti was already looking at her.

They both hastily looked away. Naomi felt heat rising in her cheeks, but before she could dwell on it too much, they arrived at the fire station.

Scotti led Naomi through to the showers. Most of the firefighters were men, with only two other women joining Scotti and Naomi in the female locker room.

Naomi swallowed as she watched Scotti starting to undress, all tan skin and defined muscles.

Maybe this hadn't been the best idea.

5

SCOTTI

Scotti tried her best to appear unaffected as Naomi started stripping. She had made the offer on impulse and was regretting it now, but it was too late to take it back. She tried not to look. Naomi had made herself clear. She wanted to be friends—*only* friends—and Scotti had to respect that.

Either she was going crazy or Naomi was sneaking looks at her out of the corner of her eye, just like Scotti was doing to her. It wasn't like Naomi wasn't attracted to her; she never would have kissed Scotti had that been the case.

No, she was holding herself back, but however

stupid Scotti thought that was, she wasn't going to try to change Naomi's mind.

Those arguments started getting thinner and thinner as Naomi bent down to wash her legs. She was facing away from Scotti, so the movement gave Scotti a perfect view of her ass. Scotti swallowed, her mouth suddenly dry.

She imagined coming up behind Naomi, bending her down even further and plunging her fingers inside of her. She wondered what Naomi's moan would sound like as she entered her.

Stop it, Scotti!

Shit, she really needed to get her head straight. Scotti's body was throbbing with desire, and all she was doing was watching Naomi's lovely body under the water and soap.

Naomi was washing between her legs now, moving further and further up. Did she really have to go that slowly? Naomi paused, and Scotti clearly saw from her arm movement that she was pressing down on her clit with her palm.

That was it—the last piece of Scotti's self-control shattered. She strode over to Naomi, nearly slipping on the wet tiles, and spun her around. Scotti expected Naomi to remove her hand at once and pretend nothing had ever happened.

Naomi did no such thing. She bit her lip as she looked up at Scotti, her hand still pressed over her clit.

Scotti raised an eyebrow. "Want some help with that?"

"Yeah," Naomi whispered. Scotti quickly replaced Naomi's hand with her own, pressing the heel of her palm down over Naomi's clit.

Naomi moaned, the sound going straight through Scotti and setting her alight with desire.

She needed more of those moans, and she knew exactly how to get them.

Scotti knelt down in front of Naomi on the wet tiles and used her fingers to spread her folds.

"Oh, fuck yes." Naomi spread her legs further, giving Scotti better access.

Scotti's tongue brushed against Naomi's clit. Naomi gasped wildly and grabbed Scotti's head, pushing her pelvis against Scotti's face.

Scotti started licking in earnest, giving Naomi the pressure she needed.

"Yes, yes, yes," Naomi chanted as she ground rhythmically against Scotti's face. Scotti had gone down on plenty of women before, but the act of giving head had never turned her on like this. She felt like she might explode with unrealized lust if she didn't get her own release soon, but she wasn't going to leave Naomi hanging just to satisfy her own needs.

The tiles were hard against Scotti's knees and the gentle spray of the shower was warm on her skin. More than anything, the slick feeling of Naomi's clit under her tongue dominated her mind. Naomi started whimpering under her breath, her thighs clenching.

Scotti knew that she was close and wanted to add to the experience in whatever way possible. She trailed a hand up Naomi's inner thigh, making it very clear where she was heading and giving Naomi a chance to stop her.

Naomi didn't stop her, didn't do anything except continuing her stream of yeses.

Scotti slid two fingers of her right hand into Naomi's pussy, twisting them around until she found her G-spot.

She knew that she had found the right spot, because Naomi stiffened and cried out, her pussy clenching hard around Scotti's fingers. Scotti kept licking and rubbing as Naomi came so hard that her legs nearly gave out.

Scotti saw her buckling and quickly grabbed

Naomi's ass with her free hand, helping to support her.

Naomi groped for the wall and pulled herself upright, panting hard.

Scotti observed Naomi, feeling thoroughly pleased with herself. It took Naomi a few minutes to collect herself and get her breath back. Scotti was afraid that Naomi would walk away—she thought she might just die if that happened. Her inner thighs were slicked with more than shower water and her clit was throbbing angrily, demanding attention.

Her hand was drawn to her clit without her conscious permission. Scotti moaned softly as she touched herself. She was so turned on that even the lightest brush of her fingers was enough to send waves of pleasure cascading through her.

Naomi repeated her own words back at her. "Want some help with that?"

Scotti opened her mouth to say yes, but a noise brought her fully back to the present. Someone was approaching, and she remembered where they were. She couldn't get caught having sex here. She'd get into huge trouble, maybe even suspended.

"Yes, but not here. My place?"

"Okay, but maybe I should drive. You seem... indisposed."

Scotti laughed. "I guess my driving right now would probably be less than ideal. Come on, I'll get my keys."

The two of them rinsed and dried quickly, and Scotti led Naomi through to the locker room. It was standard procedure for them to get the rest of the day off after a big fire or rescue, so she wouldn't get in trouble for leaving. She knew another team would have been put in place to replace them.

Scotti directed Naomi to her car and sat down heavily in the passenger seat.

"Go on. I know you want to."

"What?"

"Touch yourself." Naomi gave her a wicked grin.

Scotti moaned at the thought. The idea of touching herself like this in front of Naomi while they were driving turned her on more than it should. Scotti sat slightly lower down in the seat and pushed her hand into her pants, spreading her legs.

She had run into plenty of fires and felt plenty of heat a fair number of times before, but Scotti had never felt more on fire than she did in this moment.

She glanced at Naomi, whose eyes were on the road, but her cheeks were flushed and her grip on the steering wheel was tighter than it had to be.

Scotti rubbed on her clit faster and faster, feeling herself hurtling toward her climax at an unprecedented rate.

"Now, Firefighter Saunders, you don't want to end all the fun before it begins, do you?"

Scotti yanked her hand off her clit. Naomi was right. She wanted to come on Naomi's tongue. She'd had plenty of coming off her own fingers recently.

It had been ages since Scotti had had sex, and she wasn't going to waste the opportunity by coming in the car before she could get Naomi into the bedroom.

Naomi pulled up beside Scotti's apartment and Scotti was out of the car in a flash.

"Hurry up," she whined as Naomi took the time to close her door, and Scotti's, as Scotti hadn't bothered.

"You'll thank me later, once you realize that you don't actually want your car stolen."

"Less talking, more moving."

Naomi chuckled, but didn't delay any longer, letting Scotti lead her into the house.

Scotti was already shedding clothes, completely naked by the time they got to her room. She was pleased to see that Naomi was similarly naked, leaving a trail of clothes on the floor behind her.

Scotti practically pounced on her, kissing her ferociously, with all her pent-up lust and passion coming out into the kiss.

Naomi wrapped both arms around Scotti's waist and kissed her back enthusiastically. Scotti lifted Naomi up and carried her to the bed. Naomi wrapped her legs around Scotti's waist and didn't seem to be letting go any time soon, so Scotti got onto the bed on top of her, tightly bound to her by Naomi's legs.

She ground herself down into Naomi, feeling flames of pleasure lick through her.

"Come here. Sit on my face."

Scotti nearly choked on her own breath. It was more than she'd been hoping for, but she certainly wasn't going to second-guess the opportunity. Naomi released the grip of her legs and Scotti shuffled up until her clit was level with Naomi's tongue, tentatively pushing forward.

Naomi let Scotti know with a noise of approval deep in her throat that Scotti need not be all that tentative.

Scotti didn't need any more encouragement than that. She started riding Naomi's face with abandon, her hands clutching at the bedposts as she gasped for breath.

Scotti could feel her orgasm building and she didn't do anything to try to prevent it. She let it rip through her, crying out as she came harder than she'd ever come in her life.

She shuddered her way through it, finally flipping a leg over Naomi's head and coming to lie beside her.

6

NAOMI

It was still dark outside when Naomi turned in bed and her eyes fluttered open. It took her a moment to remember where she was —the very last place she was supposed to be- in Scotti Saunders' apartment— with her leg draped over Scotti's firm tanned waist.

They had fallen asleep naked without knowing when, both exhausted from dramatic circumstances of the day and pleasure in each other's bodies that they had ended the day with.

Naomi stared at Scotti for a moment in the dim lighting of the room. Her short blonde hair was ruffled and messy around her face. In her sleep, she looked angelic; her skin was smooth and golden brown, her chest and small breasts rising and falling rhythmically. Her golden eyelashes flickered.

Naomi found it hard to not reach out and touch her. She ran her finger softly across the side of Scotti's face.

She didn't realize when her heart began to thud and her pulse picked up the pace. When her finger ran over a scar at the side of Scotti's neck, her heart skipped a beat.

She didn't want Scotti's lovely body to be scarred and harmed. Her finger quivered with fear.

Naomi could bet that Scotti had gotten that wound on the job. She wanted to know how it happened. What happened.

Although it had surely happened a while before Naomi met Scotti, Naomi found herself worried by the incident.

What if Scotti had died then?

She fell back onto her pillow, suddenly worried. Of course she was overthinking this and she knew better, but she couldn't help but get worried by it.

She knew the answers though and the issue was that she didn't want to know the truth. Scotti was a woman who ran into dangerous situations. It was somewhat inevitable that Scotti would come to injury and harm in the course of her work.

And as much as she wanted to feign indifference to Scotti and even convince herself of that, Naomi knew that what she felt for Scotti was different from what she'd felt with others in a while. She never was satisfied with what she had with Scotti. She just wanted more and more. She wanted Scotti and wanted Scotti to herself alone.

But Naomi knew she had never really healed from her last loss. She could still remember how everything had stilled that evening after a long drawn out surgery when she was told that her patient hadn't been the only one involved in the shootout. She was exhausted already and was walking out of the office as she heard the story. There was a cop who'd gotten a bullet. But her patient had more complications and Naomi was the best to handle it. Her surgery was successful, thank goodness. But the cop, Naomi was told, had flatlined only a few moments after she'd been opened up.

Naomi was deeply sorry. Then she heard the cop's name and had crumbled right there at the exit.

Sasha.

It was only early days of their dating, but Naomi had enjoyed being with Sasha. She had loved the way her deep brown eyes crinkled at the sides when she laughed. She knew she had been falling for Sasha and Sasha was cruelly ripped away from her before their relationship ever had the chance to become more.

Naomi had struggled a lot with the loss of Sasha. She had only known Sasha a matter of weeks, so she didn't have the right to be devastated in the way that Sasha's friends and family were at her death.

At the funeral, Naomi was nobody. She was in no man's land. Just some woman Sasha had been dating before she died. None of Sasha's friends even knew she existed. She had heard Sasha's mother breaking down speaking about her hero daughter. Sasha's police colleagues speaking so highly of her. This was the woman Naomi almost loved. Would things have been different if Sasha had survived? Would things have been different if Naomi had been the surgeon to work on Sasha? Maybe.

The thoughts haunted her.

Nothing, not even what she thought she felt

toward Scotti, was enough to make Naomi think she could risk going down that route again.

At that moment, Scotti stirred and woke up. Finding Naomi awake and sitting up, she sat up too and turned on the bedside lamp. Her eyes looked darkest of navy blue in the dim light. Her golden hair flopped across her face.

Fuck, she is so beautiful.

"Are you alright, Naomi?"

Naomi nodded, putting a smile on her face and greeting Scotti. Scotti frowned, refusing to fall for Naomi's act. "I don't believe you. What's up? A patient?"

But Naomi could only think of the way she'd met Scotti. Of course, it had to be a dangerous situation where Scotti had risked her own life to save her. What if Scotti didn't get out next time she risked her life in a fire?

What if, once again, Naomi had a lover who sacrificed her life for another person?

"How bad do fires usually get before you arrive? Our fire- it was a bad one, wasn't it?"

"Sure. It was bad. Some are worse than that. Some are a lot smaller than that. It depends on a lot of stuff really. The building for one thing. Different buildings burn faster or slower. Some buildings- particularly older ones- haven't had any fire safety precautions built into them. They burn real bad. They collapse a lot too."

Naomi made a small incoherent sound.

"If you were in a situation where you had to pick between a life and yours, say, there's only enough time for one person to jump out the window of a burning house, who would jump out?"

Scotti considered the question with a funny look on her face.

"I mean, we don't tend to jump out of windows day to day... but... I came to save a life and if that's what I do before I die, I'd die accomplished."

Naomi began to shake her head. Scotti's worry lines deepened as she wondered if she didn't properly understand Naomi's question.

"I have so much experience with fires, Naomi. I have so much knowledge of fire behaviour and building construction. That person is just a victim with little to no knowledge on handling fires- how it will behave, how the building will behave. I can buy time for myself. I can come up with something. I'm a problem solver. I'm a fighter, Naomi."

Naomi got out of bed and pulled a sheet over herself.

"I'll be late to work if I spend any longer here," she said, trying hard to hide her downcast state.

"I know what you're thinking, Naomi, I know that's not what you wanted to hear."

"We can't be together! I can't... I can't... You risk your life for a living."

Scotti stood and reached out to Naomi. She put a hand on her shoulder.

"I'm not forcing you to do anything. Love forced is love strained. I don't want that for us. I'll be in your corner always, Naomi. For now, you can just be assured you're not losing me."

Naomi took a deep breath. She knew Scotti was being overly generous with her and she appreciated it. But she wondered if Scotti would always be this way, this patient. And she wondered if she could ever get past the fear she felt and give Scotti a chance. Right now it felt so much safer just to run away.

The next couple of days passed uneventfully for Naomi. She was occupied with work as usual, but her days were only filled with minor surgeries. She was on call in the evening and, instead of catching up on paperwork she needed to do, she locked herself in her office and called Scotti.

"Naomi?"

"Yes. Its me. I just. I um... I miss you. I'm on call late tonight and I'm at the hospital. I was thinking of you."

"I've been thinking of you, too." Scotti's voice was deep and to Naomi it sounded like home.

"I wondered if you had some time to talk? I've been feeling a bit lonely and I could use a friend." Naomi knew she isolated herself and was her own worst enemy when it came to friends. She didn't have many beyond the surface connections she had with her colleagues.

"Of course." Scotti said. Her voice was filled with patience and kindness and Naomi felt the tightly furled knot in her stomach begin to unfurl. Naomi knew it was anxiety and stress. Scotti was both the answer to her stress and the cause of her stress. "What would you like to talk about?"

Naomi thought for a couple of seconds, pondering her answer. "How about cars? The latest ferrari model. What color would you choose and why?"

Scotti laughed and her laughter was the balm Naomi so desperately needed. "Red, of course. Ask any firefighter you know and red is always the answer to any color question. We are just mad for red. Red for Fire Trucks. Red for Ferraris!"

Their conversation went from cars to foods and to politics. They seldom had different views, but when they did, it was fun to bicker about it.

These calls quickly became a nightly thing. Naomi chose to work a lot of extra on call night shifts- she always had- she liked to fill her time and to be helpful. Scotti, whether she was at work or at home found the time to take her calls and it was always the highlight of Naomi's day.

It was too easy to make the calls with Scotti part of her routine. Whenever Naomi took a coffee break, or wanted to break up the long nights- her phone was at the side of her ear as she listened to Scotti talk about anything and everything- as long as she wasn't on a fire call. Scotti, she learned, was a passionate talker for anything she believed in.

It made Naomi wonder what Scotti would say about her if she got the chance.

Naomi hadn't seen Scotti in a couple of weeks and they hadn't had a proper conversation about what was going on between them since the night they spent together.

Naomi knew Scotti was waiting on her to

decide what she wanted to do. The ball was in her court.

They were friends. Only friends, right?

Get real, Naomi.

Naomi knew the real reason she was avoiding seeing Scotti was because she couldn't stop thinking about how it had felt with Scotti's fingers inside her. She couldn't stop replaying the sound of Scotti's moans as she reached orgasm in her mind. She couldn't get the vision of a naked and sleepy Scotti with tousled golden hair and come to bed eyes out of her head. Naomi wanted her so very badly and she knew she would find it so hard to resist her in person.

Hence the phone calls. Phone calls were safe. Phone calls made her happy. Hearing Scotti's voice and having her in her life made her happy.

As a *friend*, of course.

The following wednesday, Naomi was called in by the chief of surgery, Dr. Agnes Frame.

"Naomi, how are you doing?" Agnes greeted, gesturing toward a seat in her office. Naomi sat in it and smiled across the table. She liked Agnes

Frame a lot. Agnes was a kind and empathetic boss, although firm, her eyes were generous. Naomi also liked that Agnes was a lesbian.

They weren't close- Naomi wasn't really close to anyone, except perhaps Scotti now. But Naomi liked Agnes, nevertheless.

Naomi wondered casually what the meeting was about, but imagined that Agnes would clue her in pretty quickly. The director hardly ever called in surgeons for private meetings. So when she began to speak, Naomi listened carefully.

"Recently, there's been several serious incidents- fires, car accidents etc in town. I'm sure you've noticed how many times we've had to work with the fire department in the past weeks. I know you have been dragged out to some of them and obviously have done some very valuable trauma work."

Naomi nodded.

"I've had meetings with the Head of the Fire Department and we had Cora on standby first notice to go out to any incidents marked as severe to assist with casualties on the scene. I noticed that you and Cora have just about the same processes in surgery. And I am sure you have noticed that

Cora has injured her ankle this week playing soccer?"

Dr. Cora Hope was Agnes's wife and Naomi always found her to be a talented trauma surgeon. She enjoyed working with her. Naomi had worked with Cora yesterday and seen that Cora was wearing a Moon Boot. She had laughed when Cora described the tackle where she had injured it.

Naomi nodded. "Cora is my preferred co-surgeon and as you know she has been assisting me on some of my research. And, yes, of course, her ankle. It isn't serious though?"

"It's not hard to see why," Agnes said with a smile. "Oh, yes, her ankle is just a sprain- it will be fine. But meanwhile, she has obviously been the trauma surgeon going out to the serious incidents. I've spoken with Cora and she thinks you're the best to replace her at the scenes while her ankle recovers. Obviously she is still working, but she won't be going out to trauma's for a while."

"Oh, well, it isn't something I had really considered. Trauma isn't really my speciality."

"Obviously, I understand that, but even so, you are the best surgeon we have and certainly the coolest head in a crisis. I think you are the best fit. Cora will handle any surgeries you have to leave behind to go to serious incidents. And while your research is on hold since the lab fire, I thought..."

"Of course. Yes, it makes sense."

"And, I heard you made friends with the firefighter who saved you."

Naomi bit her lip to stop herself from grinning. Was Agnes's question loaded or was Naomi imagining things?

Naomi nodded. "We get on well, yes."

"Then I believe this is settled, isn't it?"

Naomi wasn't sure how she felt about this. It would mean she would regularly be working with Scotti at incidents.

"If it's the best way to save lives, you can count me in."

"Great. I'll send a response to the fire department immediately and let me know that the famous Doctor Crane will be on first call for serious incidents. Thank you for your time, Naomi."

Naomi left the office conflicted within herself. She wondered if she should call Scotti and tell her or wait for the information to get to her first.

In the end, she chose the latter, deciding that she'd let Scotti wonder if it was coincidence the next time they were paired in a work setting.

The next time she saw Scotti came sooner than expected.

It was that evening when Naomi's pager beeped.

A patient coming in with the Fire Department with severe chest trauma and burns.

Naomi stood at the hospital entrance till she heard the sirens pulling in. Immediately, she ran toward it with her team.

It was Scotti who jumped out of the back door immediately as it opened.

Scotti looking handsome as ever in full hero mode. She was wearing her red fire department T shirt with her fire pants and boots. Her black suspenders were over the red T shirt. Her face was dirty and her blue eyes sparkled, she was sharp as ever. Naomi felt herself swooning on the spot.

Pull yourself together, Naomi. There is a patient here.

Naomi snapped back to life saving mode. She was a doctor. She was here to save a life.

Naomi ran to the patient as Scotti shouted the details about where they had gotten him from.

None of his personal effects had been retrieved

from the fire. They knew nothing about him except the fact that his burns were severe, there was obvious significant chest trauma from impact and he seemed to be suffering from smoke inhalation. He was already on oxygen. He didn't look good.

Naomi was assessing him as she ran with the stretcher.

The man was wheeled to the hospital on a stretcher and Naomi called out to her intern to page for further surgeons.

Scotti was standing, hands in pockets, blonde hair deliciously tousled, looking deliciously sexy when Naomi walked out of the doors into the fresh air only 10 minutes later. She scolded herself mentally for her inappropriate thoughts. She wasn't sure whether she was looking for Scotti or looking for the fresh air.

"How is he? Shouldn't you be in there?"

Naomi shook her head. "He didn't make it."

Scotti scratched her head and screwed up her face and Naomi could see how shaken by the event she was.

"You pulled him out of a burning vehicle after a collision?"

Scotti nodded sadly. "Yeah, never seen anything like it. We had it all on trying to get into the car. The door was damaged. We couldn't get him out before the fire took hold of the vehicle. He's just a young guy. He was calling out for his mom."

Naomi swore softly.

"I'm sorry you had to go through that," Naomi said. "I know how hard it is sometimes."

She was surprised when Scotti pulled her in for a hug and began to sob. It was dark and she was glad that they were under the dim lighting of the motion sensor streetlights in the parking lot.

She stroked Scotti's hair softly.

It was somewhat new to see Scotti this way around her. Between them, Naomi might have tagged Scotti the one with more emotional control between both of them. Scotti was smart and clear-headed almost all the time. It was in the way she spoke and the conversations they had. But Naomi knew well that when it came to being around life and death situations daily, there were just some losses that got under your skin. She knew Scotti felt like she had failed this man by not getting him out of the car faster. It may have made a difference, it may not. But Naomi knew how hard a loss could hit you when you blamed yourself for it.

Scotti shook in her arms and her tears fell silently. Naomi held her close.

"I know you know this, but it wasn't your fault," she whispered.

She rocked Scotti against her body where she fit perfectly. She wanted to wrap her up and kiss away her pain. She wanted to take care of her.

They were growing together, Naomi realized. What they had together was blooming. Naomi wanted to control it, wanted to determine which direction it didn't go. But she was quickly seeing how tough that was going to be.

There was something about Scotti Saunders that wasn't in anyone else but Scotti. She brought out something in Naomi. Something fiercely protective. Naomi wanted to call it friendship. But really, she knew it ran deeper than that; way deeper so much that it was almost an insult to shove what they had under a carpet and call it friendship.

But that was as far as Naomi was willing to go with it for now. They were friends, and nothing more than that.

So Naomi held her friend tight as she wept against her shoulder.

7

SCOTTI

They both trudged out of the hospital exit, barely having enough energy to lift their feet.

This seemed to Scotti like one of the longest weeks of her entire career and she was grateful for the weekend in view. Everyday of the week had dragged on unbearably, occupied by emergency calls here and there. Scotti had had to work overtime due to the immense workload.

She'd sat outside as Naomi went to work on a man they'd brought in with a heart attack that had occurred after he'd come back to find his office on fire. She didn't have to, but she'd wanted to wait for Naomi to be out. Her car was back at the station and her best way home by that time was Naomi's drive home. The surgery had lasted a while and by the time Naomi could take her hands off, it was nighttime, and the sun had set long ago.

Simply put, they both needed to unwind. Scotti was glad they were both getting the weekend off. She'd waited for Naomi to change out of her surgery scrubs and now they were approaching Naomi's car.

“I'm too exhausted to make dinner,” Naomi whined.

“I have something at home. I have drinks too. How about we go to my place? You don't have to eat alone or even think about what to eat. Sleep at my place, too, if you want,” Scotti offered. She knew they were just friends. As much as that thought made her sad, the desire to love and care for Naomi was rooted deep inside of her and friends or whatever, Scotti knew she would do whatever it took to look after Naomi in any way she could.

She could tell that Naomi was capable of falling asleep at the wheel if she drove alone as exhausted as she was. It was another reason she'd waited for Naomi. At least she'd gotten a little rest herself while she waited.

Naomi gave it a thought for less than a second and nodded. She didn't need to be cajoled at this point and Scotti's point was very valid. Scotti looked for a second at her tired green eyes and the strands of dark hair that had escaped her neat bun and were loose around her face. She might have been the most beautiful woman Scotti had ever seen.

It was Scotti who drove while they remained in an exhausted but companionable silence.

By the time they pulled into Scotti's complex, Naomi was already nodding off to sleep.

Scotti figured that Naomi may be fully asleep before dinner would be microwaved or they could have any of those drinks she talked about.

Naomi didn't appreciate being woken up after she'd fallen asleep for any reason, not even food. An emergency surgery was the only thing permitted to pull her out of bed, Scotti knew that.

Scotti, too, missed the comfort of her bed. So when they'd come in, she didn't interrupt Naomi as she dragged herself into the room and collapsed onto the bed.

Scotti, on the other hand, prepared dinner regardless, plating the meals and putting them back in the refrigerator to be heated up quickly in case Naomi woke up hungry at any point.

It was a few minutes past midnight when Scotti returned to bed and a few minutes later, she fell deeply asleep.

It was almost afternoon when either of them woke up. Naomi woke first. Famished, she went into the kitchen to find something to eat. Opening the refrigerator door, she saw that Scotti had plated up two portions of lasagne before she'd gone to bed. Naomi felt a twinge of guilt and mushiness that Scotti had even bothered.

She wanted to wait for Scotti, but her stomach was rumbling and threatening to turn her inside out.

Thankfully, by the time she'd put both plates in the microwave, Scotti was standing at the door.

Her messy blonde hair was even more undone from sleep. There were sleep marks across her cheek and she was leaning against the door with her arms folded. Her muscles were clearly defined and so sexy to Naomi. Her blue eyes looked sleepy.

The sight of her in this state made Naomi want

to go over and plant a kiss on her lips. It was exactly what she did. She couldn't resist.

She pulled Scotti into her and held her by her waist.

"Did you become a firefighter because you're already so hot?"

Scotti didn't want to grin at such a bad pun, but her lips had already spread and she had to bite them to stop herself from laughing aloud.

"That was a bad pun, Naomi," Scotti giggled.

"Want to suggest something fire?"

This time Scotti actually laughed— a sound that thoroughly pleased Naomi.

"I saw that you put out dinner. Thank you, Scotti. It warmed my heart."

Scotti blushed. She loved to be appreciated and her efforts noticed. Most of all, she liked it when Naomi herself said it. Deep within her, all she wanted to do was love and care for Naomi. Saving her life was one thing. Loving her the way she deserved to be loved was something else.

"I know we've kept dinner waiting for long enough," Naomi said, a small smile playing against the corner of her lips, "but can it wait a little longer? I got hungry for something else when you walked in," Naomi said.

Scotti furrowed her brows, trying to guess what Naomi was thinking. Naomi stood on her tiptoes and brought her lips to Scotti's and all became very clear.

"It's you I want to eat now," she whispered, and Scotti flushed.

"Oh," was all she could say, suddenly shy and aroused.

The shorts and tight tank top Scotti was wearing were, in Naomi's opinion- very sexy, and she let her know that in murmured words and the pressing of her body against Scotti's.

She ran her fingers over Scotti's right bicep. Scotti was proud of her body- she worked hard for it in the gym. Mostly she was proud of what it could do physically, but right now she was proud that it was clearly so attractive to Naomi.

Naomi kissed Scotti's ears and gradually descended to her neck. Scotti groaned when Naomi lingered. She could barely believe that Naomi was going to have her right there in the kitchen. But it was all the more exciting for the fact that Naomi couldn't wait.

"This," Naomi said as she dragged Scotti's white tank top off over her head, "is either an apology for falling asleep before dinner last night or a thank you for all the good work yesterday. Which is it?"

She covered Scotti's nipple with her mouth and suckled till Scotti began to squirm as she struggled to reply to Naomi.

"I t-think," Scotti stammered and gasped, clutching at the door and Naomi's hair, "that it is a thank you. An apology can't be this—" She moaned loudly. "This good."

"You underestimate me," Naomi said, as she went further down.

"Let's see how long it takes before you break. Hands on the counter."

Scotti didn't even realize they'd moved to the counter. She was lost in the feeling of Naomi, in the effect Naomi had on her.

She put her hands on the counter and bit her lip as Naomi parted her legs. She didn't bother to take Scotti's shorts off yet; only moved them aside with her hand before she teased for a second and then entered Scotti with her fingers.

Scotti whimpered and moaned. She could feel how wet she was with how easily Naomi's fingers had slid inside her. Naomi expertly stroked her clit with a thumb while she dug her fingers deeper into Scotti.

She opened her eyes and saw Naomi's messy dark hair half in a ponytail, her lovely eyes closed under long dark lashes as she fucked Scotti.

Fuck, she is so beautiful.

"More, please," Scotti groaned and Naomi obliged, pushing a third finger inside Scotti.

It felt so good and Scotti was overwhelmed with wanting more of Naomi. All of Naomi.

Scotti's legs trembled as Naomi's thumb circled her clit. She knew she was close and any moment now, her release would come.

She dug her fingers deeper into the wooden counter, her moans only separated by seconds now.

It was then Naomi pulled her fingers out and slid Scotti's sports shorts down to the floor. Scotti whimpered and then let out a loud moan as she felt Naomi's mouth suddenly on her clitoris. Scotti cursed and groaned as Naomi's fingers pushed back into her and began to thrust.

She was about to come, and Naomi did not let go of her tight grasp on Scotti's thigh until her efforts with her tongue and fingers earned her a loud scream as Scotti's orgasm crashed through her.

She felt herself gush on Naomi's fingers.

Only then did Naomi slide out of her, let her go and stand up to take her in her arms.

Scotti brought Naomi's lips to hers and kissed her eagerly. She could taste her own orgasm on Naomi's lips and tongue and she thought it might have been the sexiest moment of her life right there in her kitchen against the counter.

"Thank you," she said.

They had eaten and enjoyed the lasagne and gone back to Scotti's bed to lounge together.

They were barely rested when Scotti took hold of Naomi and began to kiss her some more.

Naomi was irresistible to her. Scotti couldn't think of a time before she had desired anyone this strongly.

"It's your turn now. Get up and strip off."

Naomi obliged, smiling.

"This is your punishment for sleeping when you told me you were starving."

"But I was," Naomi protested, but Scotti was already freeing her of her clothes.

"Bend over," Scotti instructed, ignoring Naomi's protest.

Naomi obeyed, curious about what Scotti planned to do. Scotti kissed Naomi's lovely back, her neck, her tattoo across her shoulder blades, down to her thighs and the backs of her legs. So many kisses for Naomi's beautiful skin.

Scotti thought she could kiss her forever. She would never ever tire of kissing her. She wanted to kiss every inch of her.

Then Scotti stood up behind Naomi who was still bent over. Bending over slightly, she felt Naomi's breasts and squeezed delicately.

With her fingers, she played with Naomi's nipples, pinching and squeezing.

Scotti heard Naomi's breath quickening and she moaned lightly.

Fuck, I'll never tire of that sound. The sweet sound of her pleasure.

Scotti noticed Naomi writhing and pushing her ass back when she touched her nipples more roughly. When she squeezed and pulled. Clearly this was something Naomi enjouyed. Naomi liked to be punished a little in sex, but pleasurably.

Scotti spanked Naomi's ass and heard her moan and raise her ass further.

She smiled to herself.

She likes this. She likes it a lot.

Scotti grabbed her hard, still pinching her nipples.

Scotti continued alternating spanks on Naomi's ass with the pulling and pinching at her nipples.

Naomi's breath was coming in quick gasps. Naomi's moans were loud and beautiful and Naomi was beginning to beg.

"Please, Scotti… I need… I need you… please"

She looked round and back at Scotti with pleading in her lovely green eyes.

Scotti had never seen a more beautiful sight.

She stepped back momentarily and could see the evidence of Naomi's desire wet and sticky on her inner thighs.

"I've been thinking of getting us a toy," Scotti said. She knew how wet the thought of it was going to make Naomi.

Naomi's responsive groan met her expectations.

"But in the meantime," Scotti said, knowing how wet and ready Naomi was. She forced three fingers hard inside Naomi curled downward slightly seeking Naomi's G spot. Naomi let out a scream that subsided to moans as Scotti began to thrust slowly and deeply in and out of her with her fingers.

She reached around and pinched Naomi's clit and toyed with it with the thumb and forefinger of her other hand.

Naomi began to shake and to moan louder. She was close.

Scotti knew she wanted to taste Naomi's orgasm.

Gently, she pulled Naomi from a bending position down to the ground to sit on her face. The kitchen tiles were cold against Scotti's back as she lay there but it only added to the moment.

Naomi squirmed and ground against her face until she threw her head back as her release came and her juice spilled over Scotti's mouth and face.

She called out loudly as she clutched a handful of Scotti's hair.

Scotti looking up and seeing her beautiful body in rapture felt like she had died and gone to heaven. Naomi's pleasure was the most beautiful thing in the world to her.

"That was so damn good!" Naomi exclaimed as she fell beside Scotti on the hard tiles.

They spent some moments there, trying to catch their breath. It was Scotti who got up first to get something to clean the place up.

As Scotti walked to the closet, she wondered

about this moment and how much it meant to her that she could do this with Naomi. She loved that she could be this way with her, but it also made her wonder how long it would continue. This was so different to anything casual and undefined she had had with anyone else.

There was still nothing defined in what they shared.

What they had wasn't something Scotti had had in a long time; it wasn't the same emotions; it didn't have the casual excitement her other relationships used to have.

This, Scotti understood, was not something she could easily replicate anywhere else.

It was Naomi alone she wanted. She couldn't fight the way her feelings increasingly skyrocketed each time she was around Naomi.

But Naomi wasn't ready for this. In fact, Scotti feared that if she told Naomi the gravity of how she really felt for her, Naomi would call everything off.

Scotti knew how badly she'd be hurt by that. In the past, she'd had casual relationships like this. None of them had ended right. The last one had gone off and gotten married to a man.

The other ones were not a better story either. They all seemed to have their lives already planned and accomplished and their relationship with her was their own stumbling block.

Scotti was used to being women's dabble into sapphic attraction. She was used to being women's bit on the side.

Scotti was used to not ever being anyone's happy ever after.

Each time, Scotti had had to deal with her broken heart alone. Something told her this relationship too was tending toward that path.

Scotti managed to hide her thoughts as she came into the kitchen and cleaned up.

Naomi had arisen from the floor and sat at the table, naked and watching her.

Fuck, she is so very beautiful.

Naomi's green eyes were glazed with lust.

"Go on a date with me," Naomi blurted suddenly.

Scotti thought she had misheard. She held the mop limply in her hand as she stared at Naomi waiting for her to repeat what she'd said.

Naomi looked shy. Her eyes darted around the room to everything but Scotti herself.

"Naomi?"

"I'm asking you out on a date, Scotti. What do you say?"

This was the first time Naomi was asking. Scotti didn't know what to say. But she knew she didn't want to turn Naomi down.

"Do you have a free day?" Scotti asked instead.

"I'll make time for us... That's if you say yes, of course."

"I'll go on a date with you, Naomi."

Naomi grinned broadly. "Alright then, let's have coffee to celebrate, shall we?"

8

NAOMI

Though Naomi had grinned when Scotti had said yes to their date, Naomi had no idea what she'd been thinking when she'd asked Scotti out.

It wasn't that she regretted it, it was that the words had escaped her mind and mouth in a moment when she was unguarded and caught up by Scotti's charm and the post orgasm haze, and now she was responsible for ensuring that the date went perfectly.

She had an idea for hotel reservations but wondered how much Scotti would prefer that compared to going to an art gallery or an exhibition like a real date. In one of their conversations,

Scotti had mentioned her love for art and for finding out the hidden messages in it.

But Naomi was interested in having a date where they could get naughty and sneak away to themselves for a moment or two. She didn't see the possibility of that being very comfortable in an art gallery considering how loudly she moaned whenever Scotti touched her.

Naomi was nervous about the date already and she hadn't even gotten past the planning stage. The only thing they had was a set date: next weekend when they were both off work. When she'd asked Scotti where she wanted to go, Scotti replied that she wanted to be surprised.

That response had raised the stakes for this date. She desperately wanted to please Scotti even though she knew deep down that Scotti would simply be pleased by anything she did with her.

It was Friday evening when Naomi finally caved and bought them tickets to see a movie. She couldn't tell why she'd settled for that option. Perhaps it was the fact that all week long, Scotti had talked about how eager she was to see the finale of a movie trilogy that was coming out. It was a romantic thriller. Naomi could not remember the last time she saw a movie, so she got them second row tickets to the movie on the release day, which thankfully fell on their date day.

Naomi picked Scotti up from work that evening when her shift finished at 7pm.

When Naomi picked her up in her Ferrari, Naomi could swear she saw someone staring at her through the upstairs' window in the Fire Station. Maybe the rumour had spread amongst Scotti's fire colleagues that she was seeing someone. Naomi wondered for a second if they knew who she was seeing. Although ultimately, she decided it didn't matter. She didn't mind.

Scotti came out of the station looking good enough to eat, clearly freshly showered wearing a loose white button down casual shirt with blue denim jeans that hugged her ass. Scotti had a strongly defined jawline. She was such a beautiful combination of the masculine and the feminine. She looked like some kind of androgynous sports model with her short floppy hair still damp.

As she got in the passenger side, Naomi could smell her. The fruity scent of her shampoo, the woody earthy scent of her perfume mixed with something else. Underneath it all, Scotti had this delicious sweet smoky smell that was just so specifically her. Naomi would know it anywhere and she loved it, the scent of her.

"So, where are we going?" Scotti asked.

Naomi reached into the backseat and took out a pair of tee shirts and tickets.

"Guess," she told Scotti as she pulled out of the driveway.

"Oh my God! These tickets and tee shirts have been sold out for weeks. How did you get them?"

Naomi shrugged, eyeing Scotti from her mirror. Scotti was beaming and Naomi was glad she'd made that happen. She was so beautiful when she smiled. She had lovely white straight teeth.

"We're going to see the new Dandelion Drive movie tonight. Those are second row seats. In case you're wondering why not the first row, you'll see."

The cinema was a fifteen minute drive from the fire station. In the car, Naomi wanted to touch her. Naomi could sense her nearness and it was both erotic and comforting. Naomi kept glancing at Scotti's denim clad thigh and her hand in her lap. Her lovely strong fingers and neat short fingernails. The things those fingers had done to her body.

Mmmmm. Jesus. Stop it, Naomi. Focus on the road.

They eventually made it to the cinema in plenty time to get checked in before the movie began.

Scotti held their Cokes and Naomi had the popcorn as they found their seats. When the cinema was otherwise full, but no one came to sit next to them, Scotti decided to ask Naomi some questions. The movie was about to begin and everyone ought to be seated by now.

"Oh," replied Naomi, "I paid for the empty seats next to us. All three of them."

Scotti furrowed her brows, "Why?"

"I don't want us distracted," Naomi responded.

Scotti wanted to probe further but the intro began to play and her attention went to the large screen.

Naomi smiled and settled into the seat. She reached her hand onto Scotti's demin clad thigh and felt electricity running through it.

The things just being close to Scotti did to her body were crazy.

The plot of the movie revolved around a woman who'd fallen in love with a girl she'd kidnapped. The instruction had been to "take care of the girl" after she dealt with the main mission, only she didn't kill the girl, she fell in love with her.

Now the gang had discovered her and she'd been instructed to right her ways. But she couldn't because she'd fallen in love with the girl. The gang comes after her, and her love and life are at crossroads.

Scotti and Naomi watched the movie, exchanging comments and reviews at intervals. Naomi found herself enjoying the movie more than she expected. At an intense shooting scene, Naomi held on to Scotti's hand tightly.

Then there was a scene when they lead characters were making out very intimately. It was exactly that moment Naomi took the opportunity to sneak her fingers into the waistband of Scotti's levis.

Scotti gasped, pleasantly surprised.

Naomi began to undo the button fly.

"This is why I didn't get the front seat and I paid for this row. This is our date. I only get a few chances to be this naughty. Keep your eyes on the screen."

Scotti parted her legs and shuffled her hips to allow Naomi access and she obediently kept her eyes on the screen.

Naomi worked her fingers inside Scotti's

underwear until she found her clitoris. She reached down further to coat her fingers in Scotti's wetness, then she used that wetness to begin to rub and tease Scotti's clitoris.

As Scotti watched the movie which had progressed to a full on sex scene, she squirmed in her seat as Naomi's fingers worked her clitoris slowly and rhythmically with a firm touch.

Naomi could hear Scotti's breathing change as she shuffled down in her seat to allow Naomi better access and Naomi loved the power she held over Scotti's pleasure.

She moved her fingers faster and she could see Scotti's body writhing under her touch. Her clitoris felt swollen and desperately aroused under Naomi's fingertips.

Scotti moaned.

"Quiet," Naomi hissed.

Naomi leant close and whispered in her ear, "I can't wait to taste you later."

Seconds later Scotti orgasmed hard and fast for her fingers.

Naomi smiled to herself. She held her fingers tight on Scotti's clitoris as she rode out her orgasm.

"I love it when you come for me," Naomi whispered and she nibbled Scotti's earlobe delicately.

Scotti's breathing gradually returned towards normal and Naomi slowly withdrew her hand from Scotti's pants.

She raised her fingers slowly to her lips and tasted Scotti's pleasure from them.

It was a deliberately seductive move and she kept her eyes fixed on the screen as she heard Scotti gasp in response.

Scotti leaned over to growl into her ear, "You just wait till I get you home!"

They spent most of the rest of the weekend in a hotel room luxuriating in each other's bodies. Naomi thought she had never felt this comfortable and also turned on by someone all at the same time. Scotti was so damn attractive, but also so kind and caring.

Naomi also bought tickets for an art gallery visit. She was glad that it that ended back in the hotel room with her head between Scotti's thighs.

With each moment together, she found out more about Scotti and opened herself up to Scotti.

It was a great weekend spent together, so when Monday came and they had to go to their separate jobs, she felt sadness deep within her at the thought of leaving Scotti and going back to work.

Something was happening inside of her the more and more time she spent with Scotti.

Her feelings were growing and she knew it. It terrified and excited her all at once.

She knew she was falling in love and she didn't know how to stop it.

9

SCOTTI

Monday started with a bang. Scotti hadn't even sat down yet when the alert went off at the Fire Station. Her heart thudded with excitement as she put on the last of her bunker gear quickly and jumped on the Fire Truck.

"Building fire far West Street. Multiple persons trapped. Doctor and paramedics will meet us on the scene." Scotti's captain briefed the team as the Fire Truck set off with sirens wailing.

Doctor? Hmmm. Who will it be?

Scotti's mind raced. Which doctor? Would it be Naomi?

Scotti wondered how bad the fire was. Persons

trapped and doctor called out usually wasn't a good sign but sometimes they were just called out for false alarms. The sirens blared and vehicles moved out of the way for the speeding fire truck.

As they sped through the city, Scotti opened her window a little in the back of the fire truck. It was something she always did on a fire call. She could always smell a fire on the wind and the distance the smell of smoke had travelled could tell Scotti a lot about a fire.

She smelled the smoke early. Thick, acrid smoke that jolted her to attention.

She began to prepare her breathing apparatus.

This was a real fire alright.

A big fire.

Scotti gasped as they approached far West Street. The fire was worse than she imagined. It had already engulfed a major part of an industrial building and it was progressing.

That was the thing about fire. It could work fast. It could devour and destroy.

Scotti always respected fire.

Fire was the most powerful mistress of all.

"Listen up," her boss said into the radio, "we don't know how many people are still inside that building. The building is clearly coming down soon. Let's get those guys out."

Scotti tightened the buckles on her breathing apparatus pack and opened the valve making the cylinder of compressed air ready for her to use while the captain gave instructions.

She jumped out of the truck with her partner, put her mask on as she moved and took a first deep breath to get the air going. She pulled her fire hood up and put on her helmet as she quickly moved to set up the hose.

She was ready for this fire.

She was assigned with her partner to the people in an upstairs room. She knew better than to take the stairs.

They immediately set up the ladder platform up to an upstairs window that seemed the best access point. The highest point of the ladder smashed straight through the window just as Scotti hoped to save her a job of breaking it when she got up there. Fire was really taking hold in the building. Flames were bursting and windows were beginning to pop out with the heat. There was a huge amount of thick black smoke.

Scotti went straight up the ladder and squeezed through the broken window with her partner Charlie. It was a lot harder to fit through windows with all your fire kit on and a cylinder on your back but Scotti and Charlie were careful and made it through. The window led to a corridor. There was a lot of smoke and things weren't looking good. Scotti knew they needed to tread carefully as if the fire was burning hard below them, the floor they were walking on could well be compromised.

They pulled a good length of hose reel through the window and tread carefully testing the floor as they went.

"Hello! Fire Department! Call out if you can hear us!" Scotti called into the smoke. The smoke was thick, and she worried that the person or persons may no longer be conscious.

She made it to the room on the corner of the building where they were headed to. The room where the people were allegedly trapped. She had to get on her knees to get into the room because the door, now nearly separated from its hinges, bent in an odd way that blocked off half the entrance. Clearly a beam had fallen from damage from the floor above.

Scotti flashed her light in every direction but it was hard to see much through the smoke. Just under the counter, she caught a glimpse of a person, hugging their knees to their chest, with a shirt held over their nose and mouth.

"Fire Department. I'm hear to help." She moved closer to what was now clearly a frightened young woman.

The woman was shaking. Scotti sighed. She knew what this was—shock. But she didn't have any time to deal with it now.

Right on cue, the door creaked, the weight of the building falling on it.

The place was about to collapse.

Scotti fixed her gaze on the woman.

"C'mon, give me your hand. We have a minute to get out of here. I'm sure we can do this."

The door creaked again. This time another wooden beam snapped.

The young lady shook her head. "I'm going to die. I'm not going to make it."

"What's your name?" Scotti asked.

"Helen," the woman said.

"What do you like most about nature?"

The lady thought for a second. "Beaches."

"Helen, if we don't move. We are both going to die. But if we do this together right now, we get a chance to see another beach. Take my hand, I know the way."

"Come on, we need to get out of here!" Charlie called already on her way crawling out the door.

Helen put a shaky hand in Scotti's. Scotti helped her stand and took off her helmet and shared her mask with Helen.

"Take some deep breaths," she said.

There was still some time to get out through the door.

She let Helen go first. "Don't touch anything. Follow Charlie. Stay on the ground and crawl till you get to that window and I'll help you down the ladder." Scotti instructed, putting her gloves over Helen's hands. Perhaps something about it gave Helen the encouragement she needed and she began to move, suddenly eager to have her life saved.

"I've got you, Helen. Follow me," Charlie called.

Scotti watched Helen until she was safely out the door and on the way to the ladder with Charlie. Scotti's hands were bare now, so she had to be extra careful. She checked once more if there was anyone else in the room even though Helen had said it was just her.

But the second Scotti took a step toward the door, the rest of the beam and the door came crashing down, bringing the fire along with it.

Scotti swore. She was trapped inside the room, she had left the hose reel outside the door foolishly and as the seconds passed, the fire was beginning to take hold.

Her eyes darted around quickly.

The window!

She ran toward it, slightly missing being hit by a falling piece of the ceiling. The window was shut. Scotti pulled a crowbar from her belt and smashed it.

She swore. She didn't have long and it was a bit of a drop. From the window, she could see Abraham, one of her colleagues. She cupped her mouth and called his name out at the top of her voice.

"Abraham! I'm gonna have to jump! Get the landing pad."

There was a big soft pad they had on the fire truck specifically for this kind of situation to cushion a jump.

He was being too slow. More debris was falling around her.

Fuck. I have to get out of here.

Through the window, she saw Helen being

attended to. For a moment, she felt relief that the young woman had made it. But the sound of something falling again brought her back to the reality she was up against.

She thought briefly of Naomi's question about risking her life to save people and her reply to it and wondered what it'd be like if Naomi heard that exact scenario is what truly caused her to die today. She shook her head as if to wave negative thoughts away.

Usually she wasn't afraid of dying.

But now, now knowing for sure she was in love with Naomi, she suddenly feared death. Death would mean losing Naomi.

Fuck.

The fire was raging now in the room. It was too hot. She felt her hands burning- she had to get out. Her fire kit could only protect her for so long.

There was only one thing to do.

Scotti clambered up the window. It was a dangerous thing to do considering that the building was falling apart and the fire was going to engulf that place any minute, but it was her only choice.

The window wasn't made of wood. It was made of metal and the heat emanating from it was intense. The lintel was hot to touch as was every other part of it.

But Scotti remained right there as the ceiling came down in many pieces. She heard something shatter and she turned just in time to see the fire lick up the rest of the room— and nearly her too.

In that second, she jumped over the window and grabbed the lintel.

The heat of it burned her palm badly but she held on, her legs swinging. The fire was coming toward her again. This time, it was going to explode and the window was going to go with it.

The burns on her palm were horrible already and she was sure she'd suffer with them for a while —if she survived this.

She spared a look down, and thought she caught sight of the landing pad, but she couldn't be sure. She was dizzy, her body weak, and her vision blurry. She knew she'd suffer later.

That is, if there was a later.

Scotti let go of the window just as the building exploded and the window blew apart.

She knew she wasn't breathing when she was falling. But she didn't know why, or if it was because she was dead.

For a moment, the world was dark and still and

she couldn't hear a sound. Then, all of a sudden, it came rushing back.

She heard someone calling her name—screaming her name, actually. She felt the surface beneath her moving.

She wondered if she'd landed on the landing pad, but she felt too tired to open her eyes.

But Scotti wasn't one to lay back. She coughed and winced as she sat up despite warnings not to.

"Scotti!"

She recognized her captain's voice immediately.

"I'm sorry, Sir," she said, knowing what was coming. "There was no other way."

The captain took a deep breath. "Your hands are badly burned. You barely made it out of there. You're going to be off rotation for awhile, so don't even argue."

"I'm sorry, Sir," Scotti apologized again. Sitting up now, she was beginning to feel the burn of her palms as her head began to pound in a terrible headache.

"We'll get you to the medical team. There's a lot of people needing immediate medical attention and there are not many doctors here. We've sent the first ambulance to the hospital. The second is ready to leave. You'll go with the third."

Scotti nodded and lay back down. A particular question plagued her mind, and she tried hard not to ask, but she just couldn't help it. Her captain stayed back, as if expecting the question too.

"And Doctor Crane? Is she here, Sir?"

The captain shook his head. "She was not one of the doctors sent with the emergency unit."

Scotti could not tell why that answer hurt more than the burns on her hand. She nodded and shut her eyes.

She was headed for the hospital either way. Naomi would see her there.

The captain tapped her shoulder lightly. "Helen told us what happened. That was a brave thing you did there. I'm proud of you."

All ride long, Scotti could not help but think about what Naomi would say when she heard she was one of the victims of the fire. She knew Naomi was going to be scared, but she hoped she could pacify her.

It was for Naomi's sake that Scotti asked to walk into the hospital herself rather than be wheeled on a stretcher despite the aches throughout her body from the fall.

Scotti didn't get a chance to walk out of the ambulance. She was still lying right there when the ambulance doors flew open. With the help of her elbows, she sat up as quickly as she could, but Naomi was already staring wide-eyed at her.

"Scotti?" she called with a stammer in her voice.

"Naomi. I'm fine, I'm fine," Scotti began to say.

But Naomi could see for herself that Scotti wasn't as fine as she claimed to be. That fact and more seemed to snap Naomi's last nerve.

It was as though the activity had ceased around them and it was just their moment. The emergency department catering to the injured victims faded away in the background, and Scotti knew that all Naomi could see was Scotti. Not just Scotti, but Scotti's burned hands, Scotti in pain.

Scotti saw tears in Naomi's vivid green eyes. She saw her pain and her fear.

Naomi turned and started to walk away.

Scotti watched Naomi's abrupt departure, and she didn't know how to feel about it. Naomi didn't even give her a chance to say anything. Didn't even ask any questions.

She felt desperate.

"Naomi!" she called, to no avail.

With some help, Scotti got out of the ambulance. She didn't head for the emergency unit as she should have; she headed in the direction she saw Naomi go.

She would have kept walking until she found her if Jeanette the paramedic, did not come after her and command her to turn around to the emergency unit.

Scotti bit the side of her lip to stop them from quivering from intense emotion. It hurt her that Naomi didn't even ask what happened or say anything other than what her body language had said.

With Jeanette's help, Scotti got a doctor to attend to her wounds. There was not much to be done other than clean them up. Thankfully, the doctor said they were surprisingly onot too deep. They would heal ok if kept clean and bandaged.

Scotti barely sat through the process. She stared blindly at the wall, her mind wandering to figure out what she did wrong with Naomi.

Well, she knew what it was. She just didn't want to accept it.

As soon as the doctor declared her free to go with her sore bandaged palms, she went to find Naomi.

Naomi, however, didn't need to be looked for. She was standing right outside the door as Scotti exited the treatment room into the ER.

"Let me see your hands," Naomi said to Scotti.

Scotti showed Naomi her bandages.

"Just minor. No big deal." Scotti said as calmly as she could.

"Screw that, Scotti, I'm the doctor here."

Naomi's voice went up a pitch, and Scotti feared that soon she'd be screaming at her right there in the corridor.

"Let's step outside for a moment. Where's your car?" Scotti asked.

Naomi didn't answer, she only led the way. They both forced their brimming emotions to stay silent as they walked out to the parking lot to where Naomi's car was parked.

They both wanted their private life to stay private and a showdown in the ER was not conducive to that.

When they made it to the car park, Naomi unleashed her anger. "What were you thinking? You could have died in there!"

Scotti fought to remain calm. "That's my job."

"Nobody says you have to die for it! You take

too many risks, Scotti! You go off script. You risk everything!"

"You're overreacting, Naomi. I don't scream at you when you spend hours standing next to a patient, trying to get them to live."

"There's nothing harmful about that. It's not like I'd mistakenly stab myself with a scalpel."

"You can't dictate to me what I do or don't do on my job, Naomi. For goodness' sake, my captain was proud of me! I might get a bravery award! I saved a life today!"

"That's what this is about? Accolades? And what happens to me then, Scotti? To hell with what I think? Awards mean nothing if you are dead!"

Scotti was beginning to lose it herself. She shut her eyes and tried to count to ten. She was sure Naomi was screaming loud enough to be heard from anywhere in the parking lot. Scotti wasn't sure she wanted their business out in the public like that.

"Look, Naomi, I'm fine. Isn't that what matters?"

"You got lucky. What about next time? What if I opened that ambulance and it was your roasted body I had to take out? You want to know what that would do to me? I love you Scotti! I'm in love with you!"

Scotti met her gaze. There were tears in Naomi's eyes and pain etched all over her face.

"I love you, too," Scotti said, without hesitation.

Naomi gave a wry smile.

"You claim to love me, Scotti? You can't say that and throw your life away like that!"

"My job is part of my life too."

"The first time I met you, Scotti, I thought you were extremely dumb to put yourself through what you did to save me. And then I realized- you had nobody close enough to you to care enough to advise you to stop all of this risk taking." She took a deep breath and took Scotti's bandaged hand gently. Scotti winced.

"The second time we met at the hospital, you fascinated me. But this part of you— the part that would literally throw yourself in the fire for anyone— it scares the shit out of me."

"I love you, Scotti. I care about you. I'm asking you to stop."

Scotti opened her mouth to talk but no words came out. She looked at Naomi blankly. She knew what Naomi was saying, and in her mind, it summed up to a decision between her and her job.

There was no answer she could give to that. She couldn’t make that promise that Naomi wanted her to. She could only stare at Naomi.

Naomi wasn't going to keep staring at her though. She dropped Scotti’s hand, turned around and began to walk away.

She didn't look back.

Scotti felt her departure like a slice through her heart and it hurt so much worse than her injured hands.

Tears began flooding from her eyes.

Naomi was the love of her life and her most impossible love.

Loving Naomi was tearing her apart.

10

SCOTTI

It was fire she ran into to save lives, but Scotti felt like she herself was drowning and couldn't be saved. She felt like she was sinking and there was nothing she could do to fight the water from her lungs. Her heart felt so much more pain more than her hands did.

If Jeanette hadn't insisted on coming home with her, Scotti wasn't sure what she would have done. She was sorry for Jeanette, who, unfortunately, was available at the receiving end of Scotti's silent treatment.

When Jeanette asked Scotti what she wanted for dinner, Scotti had said nothing, only shaking her head at intervals as if to wave away the tormenting thoughts in her head.

Later, Scotti got up and poured herself a beer. Jeanette didn't know if that was a bad idea considering Scotti's wounds and meds. But it was all Scotti had done since they returned so she let her be.

Scotti sat alone in her room— the room that, only a few days ago, was occupied by Naomi too. Now, she couldn't tell what she felt about the fact that Naomi reacted the way she did.

No, Scotti realized. She could tell what she felt.

It was anger. It was anger so intense that it numbed her.

She couldn't believe it. She couldn't believe that Naomi was more or less asking her to choose between her and her passion!

She'd wanted to be a firefighter all her life. She'd made it through a tough selection process at a time where there weren't that many female firefighters. She had had to be consistently so much better than the men only to be seen as equal.

She had worked so hard. She understood fire. She respected it. She understood buildings and how they burned. She understood people and how they behaved when trapped. She had awards for bravery. Scotti knew she was exceptional in her field. She was one of the best and she saved people. When things went really bad, Scotti found a way to save people.

And Naomi was asking her to give it up? How could she?! She was being put between a rock and a hard place. She was being asked to choose between two expressions of her love. This wasn't something she was ever going to be ready or able to give an answer to.

Scotti kicked at a chair in anger.

Did Naomi think Scotti liked dancing the tango with death nearly every day? Did Naomi think Scotti didn't realize what she meant to her?

"What was Naomi thinking," Scotti wondered. She soon came to the conclusion that Naomi must not have been thinking at all in that moment.

No thinking person would put a loved one through that.

But as Scotti said that to herself, she realized that Naomi had never really called her a loved one.

In fact, Naomi had asked that they have no strings attached.

She might have said she loved her, but love was surely not enough.

And it was because of this same uncrossable

hurdle that they remained where they were in their relationship or *situation*ship. Scotti did not know which it was exactly.

Nonetheless, whichever it was, it did nothing to wane the anger she felt at that moment.

Why wouldn't Naomi just stay and talk this out with her?

How had Naomi been able to leave her to her wounds and injuries to deal with alone?

Why didn't Naomi just realize that they were part of the job?

Scotti felt hurt to the core. Everything seemed to annoy her. She knew she was barely thinking straight but she couldn't help it.

She couldn't think up an excuse for Naomi; why Naomi hadn't even asked how she felt. Her captain had said he was proud of her, and though those words had been impactful, more than anyone else, it was Naomi Scotti wanted those words to come from.

But Naomi didn't care. All Naomi could see through her opinionated view of Scotti's profession was that Scotti had done a stupid thing in an attempt to save just one life.

Scotti signed and stretched against her bed. She was beginning to have an even worse headache and she needed to get some rest. But her mind was too chaotic.

When she fell asleep finally, she didn't know. She slept lost in fitful dreams.

The next morning, Scotti couldn't say she woke up feeling any better. She was sore all over, had a horrible headache, her hands really hurt and she was too tired to deal with anything. She couldn't even wash herself properly with her bandaged hands so Jeanette had had to help her. Jeanette thought it better that Scotti stayed at home.

“I'll go crazy if I stay in these four walls with all I feel right now. I'll get ready for work, Jean. My injury is minor and I'm off rotation anyway. I'm just supposed to be in charge of the dispatch team today. Nothing dangerous!”

Jeanette nodded. Her own house was on the next street from Scotti's, so she left to get ready for work.

“Um... thanks... you know... for helping me.”

“You are welcome, Scotti,” Jeanette said. “Please try and take it easy.” She smiled weakly as she left.

Scotti picked up her phone. To anyone else, it might have just looked like an action taken out of habit. But she couldn't deny she was hoping to find a text from Naomi. But, of course, there was nothing.

Taking a shower took longer than usual due to her thoughts and her wounds. She wondered when next she would see Naomi. Presumably sooner or later because their professional lives crossed paths with some regularity. But Scotti hoped it was later.

But her hopes were dashed later in the day when the hospital's dispatch team to the fire department arrived and Naomi was one of them.

From Scotti's office upstairs, she had a good view of the parking lot below. She knew and could see when Naomi got out of the vehicle.

Naomi was as beautiful as ever. Dark hair pulled up into a high pony, skin clear and eyes focussed, Scotti couldn't take her eyes off her.

Scotti knew exactly where to go if she really did not want to see Naomi. But Scotti realized she desperately wanted to see Naomi. Despite all she'd said and thought in her anger, she wanted to see and be seen by Naomi. If she let herself stretch her hopes, she even wanted Naomi to speak to her.

Naomi looked striking in blue scrubs that clung to her waist and curves. When she moved, it was as always purposeful, yet graceful. There was always more to the way Naomi moved that made her aura of power obvious.

Scotti was so lost in her thoughts of Naomi that she nearly jumped when a knock came on her door.

"It's open," she replied, taking out a file from her drawer. She was behind on a report she had to submit today. Luckily her fingers were able to type. It was just her palms that were sore and bandaged.

But she stopped when the person behind the door stepped into the room.

Naomi stared at Scotti.

She looked from her face to her hands. Scotti knew she did not look too good, even though she'd had two coffees this morning in a hope to pep herself up.

Naomi was quiet and watchful of her.

Scotti could only stare helplessly at her.

I love her so very much.

Naomi opened her mouth and shut it.

Scotti remained at her seat, silent and watching. Even she wasn't sure what she wanted to hear from Naomi—a worthy defense, an apology, or another scolding? Maybe a breakup? But that was only if they were ever dating in the first place.

"I'm sorry," Naomi finally said after taking a long, deep breath. Scotti's gaze did not waver. She'd thought she'd get some level of closure from those words, but they didn't come.

She leaned back into her seat and said nothing. There was an empty seat in front of her desk. Naomi didn't sit and she didn't ask her to, either. The silence between them remained tense and thick with a hundred unspoken words.

Then Naomi spoke again. "I'm sorry that I didn't get a hold of myself when I saw you. Scotti, I didn't mean to be an asshole. I just... I lost it when it was you on that stretcher when I opened the door. You see, the news of an injured firefighter had gone ahead. One of the doctors said the fire has been bad and a firefighter had literally jumped in and out of the fire to save a victim. All I could do was pray long and hard that it wasn't you, Scotti.

But it was you. And deep inside I think I knew it would be. Because only you would dare something so risky when it comes to your firefighting. I was scared, Scotti. In my fear, I didn't think clear-headedly. All I could remember was everyone else I'd lost. I'm not sure I'd be able to bear it. I'd go crazy, and a therapist and all the antidepressants in the world wouldn't be able to convince me that I'm not cursed if I lose another person to a dangerous job.

I'm scared because..."

Scotti thought she knew what the end of that sentence was. But Naomi had halted to catch her breath.

"I was scared, Scotti. I am scared."

Scotti deflated. It wasn't what she expected. But how dare she expect that when the boundaries had been clearly drawn.

Scotti took a deep breath. She didn't know what to say. She was no longer angry; she could see that Naomi really was sorry. She understood Naomi's apology too and it was enough for that situation. But Scotti feared it wasn't a permanent solution.

Naomi's fear was beyond her. It wasn't a deliberate act that she'd reacted that way when she thought Scotti was hurt. However, Scotti couldn't help but wonder what would happen if one of the days she came in really hurt from the job. What would Naomi do? Throw another tantrum and apologize later?

Scotti sighed again.

None of those questions were what Naomi needed right now. The worry on her face was palpable. If Scotti didn't take it away soon, Naomi would break down from it.

"I know you didn't mean to act that way, Naomi," Scotti said. "I thought of this overnight too. I know it's not possible that you'd ever really want to do that. It's the trauma, Naomi. We'll sort that out together. We'll find a way."

Without being asked, Naomi ran over and threw her arms around Scotti. It took Scotti a second, but she pulled Naomi in and inhaled a deep and grateful breath of her.

Naomi was her water in the desert.

"I'm sorry. I'm so sorry," Naomi kept whispering as Scotti stroked her hair.

They would have kissed, if someone didn't knock on Scotti's door at that moment. They tore apart just as Scotti's captain stepped in.

He looked from Scotti to Naomi and back to Scotti, shook his head, and said nothing about what he thought.

"I'm glad you came in to work today," he started to say, but alarm blared across the hallway suddenly.

"Emergency." Both he and Scotti said at the

same time. Scotti's body started to react to go to the Fire Truck as she had so many times before, until she remembered she was just on admin today. The other firefighters would respond.

Whatever he had been going to say was immediately forgotten as he looked to his pager for the details of the emergency.

Scotti felt torn for a second. Everything in her wanted to go to get on the Fire Truck. Her injuries weren't that bad. Could she ignore the decision made yesterday of her not being in rotation?

"Captain, I could come too?" Scotti asked, hopefully.

Though Naomi tried to hide it, there was a sad twist to her face.

"Not you, Scotti," the captain said. "You know better. Sit this one out."

Naomi looked as though she brightened up at that.

"Doctor Crane, there are casualties. We'll need you on site."

"No problem." Naomi responded, suddenly all business.

Scotti walked back to her desk, unsure how to feel.

The first emergency alarm barely ended when

the second one began to cry. Scotti sat up, surprised.

Two calls at the same time? There was no way she could sit this out.

She hurried to the pole to slide down into the big appliance room where the Fire Trucks lived. The speakers began to blare instructions. She recognized the captain's voice immediately.

"Alright guys, listen up. We've just gotten two emergency calls and almost not enough staff due to yesterday's ordeal. Fire Truck 1 and 2 will go to the house fire uptown and Truck 3 and 4 will go to the collapsing building at East Avenue."

Scotti didn't wait to find out if she could be on any of the missions. She went down to the locker room and got dressed. She winced as she put on her gloves and putting on her fire pants and boots was a struggle.

By the time she was ready and done, there were four trucks ready to leave, two per location.

Scotti's eyes scanned the groups for Naomi and for her captain.

"Scotti," her captain called from behind her.

She spun around. His eyes immediately went to her gloved hands.

"You'll be of more use at the collapsing building. Join the second troop."

Scotti nodded and jogged toward Truck 3. As the truck wheeled out of the parking lot, Scotti caught sight of an ambulance following behind. Naomi was in the passenger seat. Scotti winked in the side mirror and hoped Naomi caught sight of it.

They pulled up at the building in minutes. It was an old residential building, part of which was being used for another purpose in a way Scotti assumed ought to be illegal. Scotti marveled at how the place was crumbling, as though it had been shaken from the very foundation. The firetruck had barely come to a halt when they all began to hop out.

A crowd of people stood only a little distance away from the building as blocks fell without pattern.

It was not a safe distance, and Scotti took charge of dispersing the crowd and making way for the fire department to come through to the scene.

The building was going to collapse any

moment, yet there were people still running into it to save their loved ones and valuables.

A lady grabbed Scotti and shook her frantically. “My baby is up there! Save my baby, please.”

Scotti gave a short nod and pulled herself away from the woman's grip.

“What do you plan to do?” Naomi asked, coming up behind her.

Scotti looked at a window and saw that there was still someone in there, holding onto the drapes.

The building was too fragile to put a ladder to it. She wasn't sure if the steps could be trusted either.

“Have the crowd sent away. Put out landing pads, a number of people may have to jump,” Scotti said into her walkie talkie.

Once she received a reply, she began to move to the other side of the building to access the place better.

They had only taken a step when someone yelled from a window. “Doctor! Is there a doctor? There's a kid having seizures in here. There's no way we can get her down. The steps are too fragile.”

Naomi looked from Scotti to the window to the firefighter who had called out to her. She swore.

"Put a ladder up for me, get me in there" she said.

Scotti shook her head. "You're not going up there. We'll find a way to get that kid and the firefighter out."

"Didn't you hear him? There's no way." She knelt and opened her doctor's bag, searching for something to help. "Best we get in and stabilize the kid and get everything figured out from there."

"I'm the one with the most experience with collapsing buildings, Naomi. I'm saying, if you go up there without me you are going to get you all killed."

But there was someone already setting a ladder up to the window Scotti had said was too frail to trust.

"Please, Scotti, I need to save that kid." Naomi began to run toward the ladder, her doctors bag clunking at her waist.

Scotti swore and followed after her.

"We will take these fire escape steps." Scotti pointed to the metal steps attached to the side of the building. "I think they are safer than the ladder."

The steps shook under their feet even though they moved as stealthily as they could.

Scotti gave the building ten minutes max before it was in shambles on the floor. She wanted to be angry with Naomi for risking herself. This must have been how Naomi felt the other day.

But Scotti knew she'd made the right decision then even though it had endangered her life. But Naomi wasn't listening to her, and she was too adamant for her own good.

Scotti knew that if things got any worse, they may have to jump out of the building onto the landing pad.

That was if they were fast enough. You don't always get that much warning in the final moments before a building collapse. Well, you do get warning and they were getting those warnings right now.

Scotti took each step, fearing that if she skipped one, the building would come down. Naomi was on the last one. Scotti was on the second now. Blocks and plaster fell as she moved; sometimes as small stones, sometimes large enough to make her flinch. The pain in her hands was almost forgotten. All she could think of was getting to Naomi to protect her in any way she could.

Though it only took seconds, it felt like forever until she finally got to the second floor. There were few rooms and one of them had already collapsed. Scotti was barely thinking of other victims now. It was just Naomi on her mind.

"Naomi!" she called, without raising her voice. Scotti moved lightly on her feet till she found Naomi. Naomi was hunched over the kid, covering the kid's body with her own.

Alarm shot up Scotti's body immediately and she began to run.

"What do you think you're doing, Naomi!"

Naomi looked tensely at Scotti.

"She's alive. But she's too weak to move. We need a ladder down."

A large portion of the ceiling fell and without thinking, Scotti threw herself over Naomi and the kid. She heard Naomi whimper. Thankfully, plaster only scratched her shoulder, missing them all by less than an inch.

The window came apart from the lintel and fell inside the room.

The worst of the shaking had begun.

"We have seconds left," Scotti said. She hoisted

the kid up, cradling him to her chest. Naomi had run in without bothering to protect her head with headgear. Scotti had only two with her. One went to the kid who she picked up. Scotti took the other one off her head and put it on Naomi's head.

Naomi looked at her worriedly. But Scotti spared no time for sentiment. She heard the ladder drop.

"Run, Naomi!" Scotti ordered. Naomi hesitated but when she could not recognize the look on Scotti's face, she turned and obeyed.

Scotti ducked falling drywall and ceiling beams as she ran. Her shoulders remained hunched over the kid, her eyes on Naomi and the view before her.

"Left, Naomi!"

"Watch out!"

"Shit, Naomi! Jump!"

Her heart thudded and her breath came in heavy puffs. But she knew all of the emotions weren't merely adrenaline from the moment. It was worry, for Naomi, and passion and awe for the woman Scotti was willing to protect with her whole life.

When she sighted a weak ceiling beam about

to hit Naomi, Scotti shot to the front and pulled Naomi aside.

The exit was no longer too far. She could hear the announcements being made.

"The building is going down in seconds! Evacuate the building now!"

It was the captain speaking. Scotti wondered how long they'd stayed in there seeing as the captain had arrived on this scene.

The ceiling was falling on the steps in large thuds.

"Jump, Naomi! Jump out entirely!"

Naomi gave her best leap and came rolling down to the ground.

A second later, the building came down in a large crash of wood and stone.

It took Scotti another second to realize that she was alive and had made it just in time.

Her chest rose and fell in a heavy pants. The kid rolled weakly aside from where she had curled him up into her.

His mother and the medics ran to them, wailing and sniffling. She picked him up in a bear hug, thanking Scotti profusely. As soon as Scotti could stand without wobbling, she dusted herself and looked for Naomi.

There was only one thought throbbing in her head. It wasn't about the fact that she'd narrowly escaped death.

Rather, it was the realization that she had risked her life because Naomi had risked hers. It was the fact that both their lives were at stake when she kept watching over Naomi, sparing barely a thought for herself.

She realized she had never really felt this way toward someone.

It wasn't about the fact that they had been intimate with each other a few times and had amazing sex.

She knew what this was, even if she wanted to deny it to herself. Whatever this was, blooming between them, scared the hell out of her. Too many undefined relationships that she'd poured herself into had scarred her and taken her months, even a year, to recover.

Now wasn't the time to walk blindly into one of them again.

Yet, the way she'd thrown herself over Naomi moments ago only made one realization surface before her eyes.

The absolute fear she had felt that she never

had before in dangerous situations solidified it for her.

She loved Naomi. Not just loved but true love. Naomi was The One.

Scotti shook her head as if to make the thought fall out.

She couldn't feel that way. She wasn't permitted to.

Even though their argument over Scotti's profession was in the past, they hadn't really come to any conclusion.

Naomi never said that she wouldn't freak out if Scotti ever came back wounded again. Naomi never said she accepted Scotti's profession. And Scotti wasn't willing to give it up. Was she?

Scotti wasn't allowed to go crazy over Naomi.

And she knew that it was best she did something about this now.

Scotti saw Naomi as she came out of the ambulance. Naomi, on seeing Scotti, broke into a run. She threw her arm over Scotti and kissed her neck.

"I'm sorry, I'm sorry, I'm sorry," Naomi said into Scotti's shoulder.

"I know, Naomi. I know what it felt like when you had to run in there."

"I'm sorry," Naomi said again.

“How is she?”

“She's stable now. She’ll need tests to find out what caused the seizures in the first place. The rest of the people injured are being taken to the hospital. There's a lot of people- I need to get to the ER to help. I was thinking of taking a taxi to the hospital. Want to come?”

“Yes,” Scotti said, struggling to control the chaos within her. Naomi smiled. But when Scotti didn't return the smile, her lips turned.

“What's the matter?” Naomi asked. “Are you okay?”

“Naomi, I don't think we can do this anymore,” Scotti said.

Naomi froze on the spot. “Do what?”

Scotti swallowed, her courage dwindling too quickly.

Naomi put her hands on Scotti's shoulders. “Scotti, breathe. What are you saying?”

Scotti took a deep breath and spilled all the words all at once. “I want to be accepted for who I am, Naomi. I don't want to have to hide.”

“Hide? Hide what? We're not hiding.”

Naomi was panicking and Scotti was sorry to be the reason for it, but things like this had to be done and done early. Her mind was made up.

"You've said you love me, but you've never really committed to me in any meaningful way. My work is always likely to be an issue and I can't just give it up. You've always been skeptical about it and I'm not sure how long I can keep up with it. I know you're sorry you freaked out, but I'm not sure how many times I can keep up with it. I needed you last night. I needed the woman I love to be there for me when I was hurt. I know you apologized, but I can't help but be scared. How much longer? All I've ever wanted is to be accepted, to be told that I am loved for who I am. I can't put myself out there again for someone who is just going to end up rejecting me."

"But Scotti, I didn't reject you."

"You didn't accept me either, Naomi. I can't bear to be in between. I'll go crazy."

"Scotti, we agreed to take it step by step, remember?"

"We hoped to take it step by step. But the word was *friends*. I'm in love with you, Naomi, can't you see that?" Scotti's voice went up a notch. Naomi's hands dropped to her side.

Scotti's voice dropped a little too low. "Real love. Full on love. You are the one. You are the only one. I want it all with you. I want marriage with you. A family maybe with you. A happy ever after with you. I don't know if you feel the same for me. I can't bear to hear your answer even now."

Scotti spilled her heart out and wanted Naomi to fill it with the promises she so desperately needed to hear.

But, Naomi didn't.

"What does that mean for us then?" Naomi asked weakly.

Scotti sighed for what was probably the tenth time. It had taken her all night to ponder this idea, to muster any courage to go ahead with it, but now put on the spot, she seemed at a loss for words.

"We can't be just friends, can't you see, Naomi? It would ruin me to settle for friendship when we could be so much more if you weren't so wrapped up in what almost doesn't even matter."

"You're telling me you want to leave my life, Scotti?" Naomi said, disbelief staining her face.

Scotti nodded. She felt tears forming in her eyes as her heart ripped apart.

"It's for my own good. And maybe later, it will turn out for your good too."

Scotti was done talking. She turned around and walked briskly away from the place as if she were all too eager to be separated from Naomi.

It was the opposite actually. Scotti didn't know what she had expected Naomi to say but she knew she hadn't gotten it.

Somewhere within her as she had mustered courage to speak to Naomi was the hope that she would be wrong. Scotti hoped that Naomi would convince her otherwise or even declare her love forever for her.

But that didn't happen, and Scotti didn't want to wait any longer. More time in limbo meant the vain painful hope she held onto would be extended.

Scotti knew that if she was going to have a shot out of this, her only chance was the one she had just taken.

11

NAOMI

Naomi was livid.

Livid actually fell short of the emotion she felt. She was disappointed, upset and, well, livid! She couldn't believe Scotti.

Scotti broke up with her!

Something about that statement seemed impossible, unreachable. It wasn't something that ought to have happened between them, speak nothing of how soon it had happened.

Naomi thought there was something she wasn't understanding. Of course, it was impossible that Scotti, her Scotti, would break up with her over something as cheap as the fact that Naomi had endangered her life.

Naomi picked up her phone again to call Scotti. But she still had nothing to say to her— the words just wouldn't form.

The only word that rang in her mind was *hypocrite*. As much as she didn't want to ever call Scotti that, it was the only word that appeared to match what was going on at the moment.

Naomi itched to call Scotti, but her ego held the phone and held on even tighter to her pride.

There was no way, Naomi thought, she was going to be the first to call Scotti. It was true that they never really go defined their relationship. But that was no one's fault either, in all fairness. And yet...

How could Scotti look at her and decide they were better off without each other? Who gave her the right to make such decisions?

Naomi's thoughts revolved around questions, possibilities that could have been, and answers she guessed.

But nothing quite pacified the anger she felt toward Scotti. Naomi believed the argument had started when Scotti asked her not to go up to the child who was having seizures and she disobeyed.

Naomi wanted to scream at Scotti, reminding her that there was a kid there who would have died if she hadn't dared to go into the building. It was true that Scotti had saved her life there and Naomi was grateful for that, but if Scotti was angry because Naomi endangered her life briefly for a patient, Naomi couldn't help but call this what it was— hypocrisy.

Scotti was being a hypocrite.

Maybe it was better that it ended anyway, Naomi thought. Better now than she dated a hypocrite and faced the doom that came with it.

Naomi drove home angrily that afternoon. All drive long, though she'd set the volume of her speakers to play loudly and drown her thoughts, Naomi could not stop herself from thinking of Scotti. She didn't think she had been this angry with anyone in a long time.

It was simply infuriating that Scotti threw herself at fire everyday by the requirements of her line of work and Naomi only did it once and Scotti thought it a fair reason to sever the ties they had.

Naomi squeezed the steering wheel a little too tightly. She ought to have returned to her office and to work with the fire department dispatch team that took the injured victims to the hospital.

But after Scotti dropped the news, Naomi took a taxi home immediately. She didn't even go into her apartment. She got into her Ferrari and decided that one of those quiet drives on those lonely roads will do well for her head.

But all she'd sustained from that was a throbbing headache, a bad heartache, and a hundred contemplations without answers forthcoming.

Perhaps even worse was the fact that she'd had to deal with a pressing truth: As mad as she was with Scotti, the only person who would know what to say to her in a mood like this was Scotti herself.

Too many times she'd picked her phone up, even twice dialed Scotti's number and dropped it. All she had in her was a rant, and a rant wasn't going to do anything for either of them.

Naomi wanted Scotti. She craved nothing more than Scotti's touch. It was Scotti's voice she wanted to hear again desperately. But before she would ever hear that again, she had to be ready to say that she did not care if Scotti endangered herself a hundred times a day to save someone else.

Naomi could not bring herself to lie like that. Even if she somehow managed to knit the words together, her very body would betray her real thoughts.

Naomi turned to the next street.

It was getting too late to still be out here driving around. The road was eerily quiet and it had been a while since Naomi passed another vehicle. She knew she ought to turn around and go home, but the thought of meeting an empty home feeling this way was depressing.

It brought a memory back to her mind; the night she'd returned home after receiving news of Sasha's death. The house had been so silent, Naomi could hear her own crippling thoughts aloud and was paralyzed by them.

She feared that this moment bore a strong resemblance with that one and that she'd immediately go down that black hole again.

It was best that she drove the night away, paying attention to its sounds and whispers and begging them to take away her looming depression.

The next morning, Naomi arrived at work with the telltale signs of her sleepless night hidden under layers of foundation. Her smile was a little too bright and her hands shaky.

She was already having a horrible day in her mind when she got the instruction that she was to go with the dispatch team to work with the fire department.

Naomi couldn't recall if it was Scotti's team on duty or not; she hoped not.

But who was she kidding?

The team waiting for the doctors was headed by none other than Scotti Saunders. Infuriatingly handsome in her red fire department shirt. Her eyes were almost navy blue and hard to read. Naomi rolled her eyes.

Why didn't Scotti just stay at home for one bloody day and nurse her wounds?

Naomi couldn't believe that she didn't even know what Scotti's burns looked like. Between the argument and the bandages, she hadn't had chance to see them. She wanted to examine them and clean them and treat them herself. How could she possibly trust that to anyone else? She hadn't even gotten the moment to kiss Scotti's pain away.

As Scotti approached them now for a quick greeting, Naomi's gaze dropped to Scotti's gloved hands. She itched to tell Scotti off; to tell Scotti that her burns needed some time to heal before being subjected to the discomfort of the fire-fighting gloves again.

As usual, Scotti extended a hand for a shake to each doctor that had come to help. When it was time to shake Naomi's hand, Naomi thought Scotti dropped her hand too quickly. Naomi wondered if, in her desperation, she had squeezed Scotti's hand too tightly.

"There's a road accident scene we'll need to take care of, guys. The hospital is needed and the tow trucks are unavailable. There's no time to waste, it's a major road," Scotti barked.

Naomi couldn't look at Scotti— wouldn't look at her. Whereas she usually sat in the front of the truck with Scotti, Naomi now ignored the seat and found one further away at the back. She even considered taking her own car.

She needed to be as far away from Scotti as she could get. As long as she still saw Scotti, Naomi was convinced that a conducive environment for healing was merely an illusion.

She tried to reduce their conversations to monosyllabic replies and said them only if necessary. But she couldn't cheat her mind, and many times she caught herself staring at Scotti or touching something Scotti touched for too long.

Naomi wondered if Scotti felt the way she did; if Scotti even noticed she was gone. Scotti seemed to be handling it better than she was. Scotti met her eyes with professionalism, whereas Naomi could barely look at the ground where Scotti stood. She hid this by looking at the patient instead or her report booklet or her phone.

She watched Scotti steer oncoming traffic away to another lane as she and the rest of the team handled the accident victims and cleared off the road.

That was only the beginning of the many paired missions they had together. Naomi wondered if fate was playing a cruel trick on her. Sometimes, Naomi thought that their pairing was just unnecessary.

It was agony that she was so close to Scotti, sometimes even physically touching, yet they were so far away.

She missed the moments when she and Scotti would sneak away at the end of a mission to talk alone. She missed the conversations she and Scotti used to have on the road.

Naomi wondered if the difference was obvious to everyone else and they were just pretending. Did they notice the rift between what used to be the best pair on the job?

Naomi tried as hard as she could to see that her job didn't suffer the brunt of her loss, especially when she worked with Scotti. But she could not help but realize how quickly Scotti seemed to snatch her hand away when an opportunity loomed for them to touch.

Even though there was once a time Naomi had only known Scotti as a dedicated firefighter, Scotti's professional tone seemed too unusual to Naomi. Sometimes she wanted to scream at Scotti to just stop.

It annoyed Naomi even more that Scotti didn't see or appear ruffled by the obvious torture she was going through. And dear God, Scotti hid hers too well.

One time, it took Naomi all the self-control she could muster, not to grab Scotti by the collar, pin her to the wall and kiss her silly.

She'd fisted her hands and dipped them in her pockets to avoid creating a scene.

It was also that day that Naomi decided she

was going to request that her pairing with Scotti be dissolved.

She thought it up in her head and cooked up a seemingly reasonable explanation that put neither of them in the center of the story on why she needed an immediate change.

They'd made a good team in the past. They'd saved more lives than Naomi could have done alone. In all honesty, she knew she'd miss the team they were. But if Scotti thought it was best that they severed the ties now, they better sever all of them.

When she got on the firetruck with Scotti once more, she believed it was going to be the last time. Perhaps, it was going to be the last time in a long time that she would see Scotti. Naomi thought she was ready for it.

If this was healing, then so be it! she said to herself.

Naomi arrived at the scene a little later than Scotti had because Scotti had gone with the first dispatch truck.

She found Scotti bent over a little girl, gently treating a burn. Naomi felt touched seeing Scotti in such a way. Scotti was unaware that she was being seen.

When she saw Naomi approaching, she said, "Here comes one of the best doctors you'd ever see. She's here just for you."

For some reason Naomi couldn't explain, hearing Scotti say that took her back to one of their missions when they'd tried to save a lady who had hyperventilated until she had a heart attack.

Naomi had refreshed Scotti's training on how to do CPR that day.

Another time, Scotti taught Naomi how to skillfully scale a ladder in case of an emergency. All lesson long, Naomi had done more staring at Scotti's well-shaped ass than actually concentrating on what Scotti said.

Naomi crouched next to the little girl. "How did you get one of the best firefighters in the world to focus just on you? You've got to have some powers I don't have."

The little girl giggled. Scotti stood, winking at the girl.

To Naomi she said, "You take her on from here, I'll go to the others."

Naomi nodded. She wanted to tell Scotti that she meant what she just said to the girl. But that was just going to be poking at a wound that was only just starting to heal.

By the end of the mission that day, Naomi sat at the back of the last of the firetrucks that exited the place. The truck was being driven by Scotti. It was another thing Naomi found painful about Scotti leaving; she didn't get to see Scotti behind the wheel of her Ferrari anymore. She missed the confidence and daredevil aura to which Scotti commanded her car. Before Scotti, Naomi loved her car for its looks most of all. But Scotti had come and owned it from the first day as though the wheels were an extension of her hands.

On the mission that day, it dawned on Naomi that dissolving her pairing with Scotti wasn't just robbing herself of good memories and experiences with Scotti, it was robbing the world of things too. Agnes Frame was right; Scotti and Naomi made an awesome pair— one no one had figured was needed until it was made. The lives they saved and would later save was worth it more than Naomi's personal gain.

Healing wasn't going to come in dissolving the pair, Naomi told herself. Healing was going to come if she chose to heal.

That evening, when she sprawled her exhausted body across her bed, Naomi let herself decide that it was time to heal. If she was going to be a good doctor and also hopefully soon get back to her research, she had to deal with her own issues first.

On the top of that list of her issues was getting over Scotti as soon as possible. She missed nights when she didn't have to worry about a significant other. Such a time felt like ages ago.

Naomi didn't know if she was shutting herself off relationships entirely, but she was sure of the fact that if the universe was going to keep sending her love in the hands of a person who was a ticking time bomb, she'd rather stay away.

Before she slept that night, she booked an appointment with a therapist who was running some clinics in the hospital.

Dr. Barb Skye was already seated when Naomi walked in early the next morning. They had worked together on some cases before. Dr. Skye was an experienced psychologist who had many skills and was currently doing some clinics with victims of trauma. She had to be about 60 years old and she was a very wise head.

Naomi liked Barb. She liked her no nonsense talking, she knew Barb was also a lesbian. She hoped given these facts that Barb might be able to help her.

“You know, when I saw that email from you, I thought it was a very good internet scammer who'd gotten a hold of my email. I nearly ignored it from disbelief.” Barb cackled to herself.

“Good morning to you too, Doctor Skye,” Naomi said, taking a seat.

“I'll have to leave 20 bucks at Harry's for losing this bet. I never thought I'd see you here.”

“Not everyone needs a visit to the therapist, Barb.”

Barb raised her eyebrows.

“I may beg to differ on that one,” she said.

“So, what brings you here?” Barb pulled out a file and scribbled Naomi's name. She looked up at Naomi, who had still said nothing.

Naomi looked from the flower vase on Barb’s table to the painting behind her. Then she raised her head, surprised at how quickly tears came to her eyes.

Barb said nothing, only handed her a tissue.

Naomi dabbed her eyes and sniffled. Barb waited patiently, it would be no surprise to her how quickly their lightness had taken a turn.

She knew Dr. Crane as a strong-willed woman who always put up a firm emotional front. She would no doubt wonder what made Naomi Crane cry now.

Naomi took a deep breath.

"I ruined it with my girlfriend," Naomi blurted.

Barb fixed a knowing gaze on her.

"Well, she wasn't officially my girlfriend. We were.. well... we were something... I loved her. Love her. I love her. But it isn't to be."

Naomi had no idea how to put it into words.

"It's the handsome blonde firefighter, isn't it? She saved your life and you fell in love with her."

Naomi looked like a child caught with her hand in the cookie jar. She gave a small nod.

"I want to forget about her and move on," Naomi said.

Barb raised an eyebrow. "Honey, I'm a therapist not a genie."

Naomi rolled her eyes.

She'd always admired Barb. Not romantically, but as the type of person she imagined she could easily spend a good day with.

"I want to live happily on my own. I'm tired of my heart skipping each time I smell Scotti's scent. I'm tired of being unable to meet her eyes, I'm tired of being angry with Scotti."

"Tell me about you and Scotti, Naomi."

Naomi launched into a detailed story immediately as though she'd recounted it a hundred thousand times to herself and had only been waiting to be asked to say it aloud.

She told Barb of how they had met and how they'd immediately hit it off. She told Barb of how Scotti shared her passion for cars and how she became a firefighter because as a kid she was fascinated by fires.

"Damn, Naomi. The way you talk about Scotti, that isn't someone you need to move on from and forget."

Naomi sighed.

"Scotti is too good for me. Scotti doesn't care about her life when others are in danger. That kills me with worry. Scotti is too much of a superhero for me to keep up with." Naomi paused. "Enough about Scotti. Tell me what to do."

"You're doing exactly what you need to."

"Will I be able to get over Scotti? I don't want to have to not work with her. But working with her and pretending I'm not absorbed by my feelings for her is impossible."

Barb leaned back into her seat.

"Tell me about Sasha," she said.

Naomi's body stiffened visibly.

This was the hard part; Barb obviously knew her history.

Sasha. Lovely Sasha with her infectious laugh and her calm composure. Why did Sasha have to die? Why did Naomi never really get her chance with Sasha? She never really knew her. Sasha was young and smart, capable and beautiful. How could life be so very unfair?

"I never got chance to fall in love with Sasha. She managed to go to work and get shot before I got chance."

Naomi sighed deeply.

"It feels so very unfair. She should have had more chance at life. I should have had a chance with her. But, I'll never know if it would have worked between us, because she was killed before I could find out."

Barb looked at her over her glasses, knowingly.

"And you haven't grieved the loss of her."

"How can I grieve for someone I only knew a couple of weeks? I went to the funeral and nobody even knew I existed. I didn't know what her favorite song was or how she liked to eat chinese food when she was stressed. How could I be entitled to any grief for her?"

"You shared something with her before she died. You shared time. You shared your bodies. You shared feelings for each other. Tell me what you liked about her."

Naomi could vividly see Sasha still in her mind.

"I loved her smile and her laugh. I loved the way she would tease me about how serious I can be. I loved how it felt when she wrapped me up in her arms. I actually loved her passion for her job. Her passion for helping people. We shared that. I share that with Scotti, too. But I just can't get around to loving Scotti's passion for her job. Scotti's passion for risking her life."

"Is Scotti's passion actually for risking her life, or do you think Scotti's passion and in fact Sasha's passion are actually both just that they want to help and protect people? Their passions might be that they just care too much?"

Naomi thought for a second and nodded. "Scotti cares so very much. She is so gentle with people she helps. I do love that about her. I love watching her work with kids."

"Tell me when you recovered from your loss of Sasha."

"Tell me when you'll ever stop being totally nosy," Naomi quipped. Barb remained silent. Naomi hissed. "A person just ends up healing, Barb. Time, time, time. It heals, it numbs. Anyway. It wasn't my loss. Sasha wasn't mine to lose."

"Do you honestly think you're numb or healed?"

Naomi rolled her eyes again.

"Is Scotti yours to lose? Even if you separate from her. Even if you move on? The bit that is yours to lose is the love that you share. You love Scotti. You loved Sasha. You loved things about her. You enjoyed being with her."

Naomi shrugged.

Barb continued, "tell me that you requesting this session with me is honestly about you living alone happily. Tell me you're not hoping that something changes about you so that you can go back to Scotti and find a way through this."

"Are you here to state the obvious, read my fortune, or fix me." Naomi looked at her wristwatch in frustration.

"It's almost time for your clinic," she said, drily.

"My clinic isn't for another hour, Naomi, and you know that."

Naomi leaned into her seat. "What are we going to do?"

"We're going to work on dealing with loss."

Naomi stared into space without saying a word. Barb kept quiet and watched Naomi.

Naomi nodded slowly. "Okay."

Barb smiled, smugly.

"I can see you again on Wednesday and Friday this week and then we can sort out some regular sessions going forwards."

"Send the timings to my email and I'll try my best to meet them," Naomi said, standing.

"You'll be glad you're doing this, Naomi. I can't guarantee that there's more for Scotti and you. But you need to do this for yourself. You need to grieve and heal yourself in order to move on in life, if you stick with this, there's hope."

Naomi was at the door now. "If life gives me another girlfriend in a dangerous profession, I'll be sure I'm cursed."

She shut the door behind her as she walked down the corridor lost in thought.

All day long, Barb's question remained on her mind. Not necessarily because Barb had asked to be told about Sasha, but because in that moment, Naomi had realized that she was never really over Sasha. Not as a romantic partner- who knew if it would have worked long term- but as a part of her life that death had snatched from her. They had been happy together. They might have continued to be.

She'd realized there and then that had roots with what happened to Sasha the night Scotti hurt herself.

Naomi wondered if there was a possibility that a time would come when she won't have to overthink Scotti's profession or that one day Scotti would leave her home and she wouldn't be frightened that would be the last time she saw her.

But again, being in therapy was no assurance that Scotti would come back to her. In fact, they hadn't spoken personally since they broke up. Naomi feared that Scotti was quickly forgetting her, moving on like they never were.

She, on the other hand, was stuck, like a song set to repeat.

She saw Scotti, in her opinion, too many times a week. But like an addiction, she was happy to have that many times to see Scotti no matter what it did to her healing process.

By midday, her phone beeped and she received Barb's email. Therapy was set to start Wednesday, the same time and the same place. Naomi didn't stop to wonder if she was really ready to let go of this part of her that had been there for possibly longer than she was even aware of. She sent a reply to Barb assuring her that she would be there.

Barb was doing this to help her, she knew that. Barb hadn't been joking when she'd said she'd been in the office earlier than usual for Naomi's sake. Now Barb was going to be doing this for quite a while. Naomi told herself that it was for this reason that she'd show up for it.

It wasn't an entirely true reason but until she was mentally healthy enough to face the truth about herself again, she'd let herself use Barb as an excuse.

Naomi was seated in Barb's office early wednesday morning. She watched as Barb made coffee before coming to sit.

"Surprised I didn't change my mind?" Naomi quipped.

"No. This isn't the part where you wonder if you've made the wrong choice." Barb didn't give her a moment to think over the statement; she continued immediately, "Let's get busy."

"Tell me how you met Sasha," Barb began.

Naomi's eyes roamed the room briefly as she gathered her words. She took a deep breath and started before stopping abruptly. This wasn't something she'd ever talked about since Sasha died.

She'd told Scotti about Sasha, but she hadn't gone into the details of it. What Barb was asking her to do now was somewhat different. Barb wanted her to reach into the depth of her mind and reach into memories she'd shoved away from her chest so that she could breathe again.

She reached out and took the cup of coffee Barb had offered her. She let the warmth go through her palms and let her mind gather what she needed to say.

"When I bought my Ferrari, I didn't want to

take it everywhere. For most of the time I had it in the beginning, it was parked at my house. One day, I found out about a street that no-one really knows or uses. I'm not sure why. It seemed a good place to give my car a ride. For some reason, I didn't think I could get hurt there or that the road was sealed off or something. But I rode there that evening and the next day and the day after."

Naomi's gaze was fixed on the cup and nothing else; as though from there, she conjured tales of how she'd met Sasha. When she paused, she took a sip of coffee. She'd requested it black, without sugar. Naomi rarely took coffee except on days when it was too cold.

Today wasn't one of those days, but she thought she couldn't do without the beverage in her hands.

"One day, I got pulled over. I wasn't speeding and I was the only car on the road. In fact, I was surprised to see that there was a cop there at all. When I stopped, it was Sasha.

She's was the kind of woman that makes you lose your breath on first sight. She was tall and striking with these lovely brown eyes and clear brown skin. She looked like some kind of model. We used to joke that she made me lose my breath and I made her lose her words. She was going to ask me a number of questions, but she stuttered at her first word. She apparently already knew who I was and said Dr. Crane and I was surprised. She said she'd been at the hospital a number of times and everyone knew who I was. I'd never seen her before. I used to wish I had met her so much earlier. We could have had more time. Apparently, she was on a patrol that day and figured out that someone had reopened that road. It's a cul de sac kind of a road, a long drive to the end of a mountain.

I asked to get her number just in case I ever needed it. I... Do I really need to keep telling this story, Barb?"

"You can take a break if you want to."

"We have less than five minutes left. I don't have time for a break," Naomi snapped. She stared at her cup of coffee.

Naomi finally tore her gaze from the cup and fixed a dry look on Barb.

"What is talking about meeting Sasha going to do for me?"

"You forget too easily that I'm not any random therapist whose office you just walked into. We've known each other in some capacity for years,

Naomi. We've worked on the same patients sometimes even. So, when I think that I know you, I'm basing nothing on assumptions and fallacies. I know you, Naomi. This is something you've always needed to talk about. Death only stole the emotions with which you wanted to convey your story about Sasha. This conversation is me telling you that you can have that back."

"I think I'm done telling you about meeting Sasha," Naomi said softly.

Barb let the topic lie where Naomi left it.

For the sake of both their jobs, each session was set to go on for thirty minutes. Naomi felt like this was the longest thirty minutes of her life and now she was suddenly a little too eager to go.

She stood and walked toward the door.

"Let's do this another day, Barb."

Naomi left the room mentally exhausted and wondering how she was going to get through the rest of the day.

But two hours later, she was sent to work with the fire department.

Naomi hadn't sat by Scotti in quite a while, and she didn't dare it today. Inwardly, she dreaded the day Barb would require that she spoke about Scotti. Naomi wasn't sure how she'd survive that

12

NAOMI

It felt as though so much time had passed since Naomi started therapy. But when she looked in her calendar, it was only going to be a month in two days. Nearly a month of consistent therapy for at least three times a week.

The night was dark and too silent for Naomi as she laid in her bed. She would have turned on music but when she had done so earlier, it sounded like too much noise. She'd tossed and turned, and her bed was undone for what was the third time that evening. She got up, tucked it all in once again and laid back down.

Barb had told her that taking deep and steadying breaths were helpful. But she'd taken many tonight and the last thing it seemed was helpful. With each exhale, she felt like she was losing it and with each inhale, she wondered if this was the moment her heart gave way, exhausted from being compressed with breaths she wasn't sure she wanted anymore.

This unbearable feeling had started when, earlier that day, she'd arrived late to the dispatch truck and there had been nowhere else to sit, save in front with Scotti.

In that second, Naomi had tried to think up any reason, even ludicrous ones, why she could not sit there with Scotti.

But they were already a minute late for an ongoing emergency and any other delay was cruel. She hopped onto the truck and sat still the entire journey.

Every emotion had run through her in those few minutes she sat there. However, the most highlighted ones were desire toward Scotti and anger at Barb. Anger because when she'd sat next to Scotti, she hoped that her emotions toward Scotti had died off during therapy. She'd hoped that her many sessions of confronting and sitting face-to-face with uncomfortable emotions had changed her in the way that she needed the most.

But when her heart had skipped each time that Scotti's hands moved on the steering wheel, she'd realized it wasn't so easy. Scotti had caught her one too many times staring at her, and her navy blue eyes looked confused and it made Naomi wonder what kind of a fool she must have looked like, drooling over someone who didn't want her anymore. When Scotti had run into the building that was only beginning to seriously go up in flames, Naomi had stifled the urge to run after her for protection.

At that moment, Naomi had flared up inwardly at the realization that nothing had truly changed. Everything she felt toward Scotti was still the same, if not even worse.

She'd stomped into Barb's office without permission later that evening. It was a few moments before closing time, but Barb let Naomi sit down for the conversation she looked like she desperately needed.

Naomi began practically yelling, her voice pitched higher than her natural tone, scolding Barb. Midway, she'd burst into tears and Barb hadn't done much more than offer a tissue.

She'd listened to Naomi sob about how she expected that she'd be fine in a month or at least have some improvement. She'd said nothing as Naomi questioned her on why nothing was working.

Barb sat on the other couch as Naomi cried.

Barb waited until Naomi's sobs had reduced to occasional whimpers and wheezes before she stated that, in truth, Naomi was making a lot of progress, even though not as quickly as Naomi had expected.

As soon as Naomi had managed to pull herself together, she got to her feet and left without another word to Barb. She'd gone straight home.

Her house had never felt as empty as it did that evening. Everything seemed to echo and seemed like too much noise.

She didn't bother making dinner after she'd tried to get leftovers out of the refrigerator and there was nothing she could decide on. She couldn't eat mac and cheese without reminiscing on one of their dates when Scotti had spilled her mac and cheese wailing over a movie character's death she thought unnecessary.

The only other thing in the refrigerator was bacon and eggs and juice. The emptiness of it all today weighed down on the memory she had of Scotti always having something for her to eat by the time she came home. Scotti always meal prepped nice meals. She always had something nice in her fridge.

Naomi had trudged to her room and laid in her bed where she remained until night came.

She needed sleep tonight. She was too stressed not to have any. She'd had a busy week; in and out of the hospital, in and out of the fire department, and coming home to nothing exciting. She was exhausted to the core and sleep should have been awaiting her by the time she got to her bed, but insomnia was all that wrapped arms around her and stole even the blinks from her eyes.

She was left alone to her thoughts and worries. What if therapy was not the solution for her? What if she never got over this fear? What if she really died without anyone to miss her?

On and on her fears continued to climb, until she had to sit up to stop herself from hyperventilating to death.

Therapy was not going as fast as she envisioned. In the sessions, she'd told Barb just about everything. It was easier to talk about those experiences with time. There was even a time she let herself laugh again over a funny experience she'd had with Sasha. Barb told her that as soon as processed and grieved Sasha's death, it was going to be easier to deal with whatever stumbling block there were between her and Scotti.

There was also another day when Barb had been stern to her. She'd told Naomi that if she didn't want to get better, she shouldn't have started in the first place. Naomi had wanted to put up a fight, but she knew Barb was right. So, she'd sat back and given it another chance.

Perhaps it was for all those reasons that she was so upset with what happened today.

Barb saying, "Give it time. Give yourself time," rang in her ears.

How much time was too little time and how much time was too much time?

What if by the time she was fine, there would be no hope for her?

Right on cue, her mind reminded her of Barb urging her to trust the process.

"No one is promising anything immediate, Naomi. If you want a change in a couple of days, you may want to go back home and save your money. But if what you want is true healing, then, that, I may be able to offer."

Naomi waved off Barb's voice plaguing her

mind and reached for her phone on her bedside table.

There was only one contemplation topping the rest of her thoughts at this moment. She turned the phone over in her hand a number of times, feeling the flat surface. With a click to the side, it came alive.

Naomi clicked the contact button and turned the phone off again.

Her glow-in-the-dark clock said that the time was some minutes to midnight. Naomi wondered what Scotti would be doing at this time.

If she had a long day, she'd be asleep by now. However, she'd been with Scotti for most of her workday. She didn't think the day qualified as a long day. It was one of those kinds of days when they still had enough energy afterwards to grab dinner or go on a date or get home to have fun.

Naomi believed that Scotti would still be awake if she called. She toyed with her phone for a couple of seconds more, then, taking a deep breath, she turned it on. She scrolled nervously till she found Scotti's number.

She clicked it nervously, barely looking at the phone. She turned it over as the dial began to buzz rhythmically. She tapped the side of her bed with nervous fingers. The phone rang for too long. Then it stopped, and Naomi let out a breath she hadn't realized she was holding.

It wasn't a hot night, but beads of sweat had started to gather at her forehead. She didn't bother trying a second time. That kind of courage she'd just mustered was an act of desperation; it didn't come twice in a row.

Naomi left the phone lying there as she laid back and forced herself to sleep.

Maybe she would have fallen asleep from embarrassment and exhaustion if her phone didn't ring nearly thirty minutes later.

Naomi shot up from her bed, nearly losing her breath and balance.

There could only be one person calling that number. Sure, it could be a work-related emergency, but then they would have just paged her, surely.

Her hands shook as she reached to pick up the phone. The words dried from her mouth and throat as thoughts of all the things she wanted to say to Scotti disappeared from her mind.

The ringing was nearly coming to an end when she finally answered it, only glancing briefly at the caller.

There was silence for a moment on both sides as her heart thudded frantically. Finally, it was Naomi who said, "Hello," in a voice that was too foreign to have come out of her.

"Hello?"

Naomi froze, nearly dropping the phone.

The voice that replied wasn't just strange, it was deep and male. That wasn't Scotti's voice.

In that second, a thousand and one things that could be wrong ran through her mind. Had Scotti gotten hurt on her way home? Was Scotti trapped somewhere?

And most of all, who was this man with Scotti by past midnight?

"Scotti?" Naomi called with a shaky voice.

"Doctor Crane?" the male voice responded. Maybe it was because it suddenly sounded too familiar that she pulled the phone from the side of her face and checked the number.

Her heart dropped to her stomach.

"Ah shit, I'm so sorry, Scott. I didn't mean to wake you or dial your number."

Naomi slapped her forehead. In her unease, she'd dialed a wrong number. Scott Sanders was a man she'd worked with on a project a while ago and an employee of the hospital where she worked.

She was still apologizing profusely when she heard a muffled conversation. She swore as she remembered that Scott was married.

"I'm sorry, Scott. I was trying to reach someone else," Naomi said and hung up. She tossed her phone away from her and it bounced to somewhere her eyes didn't quite catch.

She couldn't stop swearing. She was going to have to apologize to Scott again the next day. Hopefully, his wife thought nothing of what just happened.

This occurrence was enough drama for Naomi for the night and she told herself that if she was wise, she ought to lay down and wait for sleep to cover her embarrassment and anxiety.

She chided herself for not checking the name properly, for being too anxious and too frantic. She told herself that she was being too wishful to think that anything would make Scotti call her back, especially at this time of the night.

It was with that thought that she fell asleep and didn't stir till morning.

13

SCOTTI

Scotti got up exhausted the next morning. She had barely slept a wink until the sky had begun to lighten to welcome the day. All night long, she'd binged on television and comic books. The result was that she felt like a ghost of herself by the morning and could barely remember anything from the night before; not even what she'd thought of the movie or book.

It had been like that for weeks. She'd come home as late as possible to avoid the emptiness of the house. Then she'd turn on the TV for the sake of company. She only ever watched the shows or movies with less than half attention. Sometimes, if she was lucky, she'd fall fast asleep a few minutes past the introduction.

But it was unlike Scotti to sleep during a movie. She loved them, especially sci-fi or anything that showed off an array of cars. But since she and Naomi had broken up, Scotti had barely looked twice at a car—as though that was what was really the issue.

In Scotti's opinion, the best dates she'd had over art or cars or movies were the ones she had with Naomi. It'd been too hard to try to recreate the experiences alone. She'd tried, but perhaps it was all too new and raw for her to stand them. Soon, even the movies she saw at home alone turned to background sounds that she slept to.

Last night was quite different. She'd turned on the TV and put the volume low, but nothing like sleep had made a pass at her all night.

She'd drunk two glasses of warm milk but that did nothing for her either. Later, she scrolled on Tiktok for hours. She'd not even dozed off for a second. Her eyes were wide open, even after she put her phone down and stared at the ceiling.

Scotti knew where this difficulty had started. In fact, the minute the passenger door had opened and Naomi had hoisted herself up to the seat,

Scotti had known that sleeping that night was going to be difficult for her.

When she'd broken up with Naomi, Scotti wasn't sure she'd been expecting this—the sleepless nights, the inability to breathe when Naomi was inches close to her or the way that her thoughts constantly punished her for her decision.

In truth, she hadn't expected an easy road either. But this only told her how deeply in love she'd been with Naomi.

Scotti had thought she'd caught the feeling when it was young and new. But in the days that followed after her breakup, Scotti realized that this was a feeling that ran deep into her very person. It was a feeling she could not easily put aside just because she had detached herself from the source. If anything, Naomi was all that occupied her thoughts the most.

It'd been over a month that they went their separate ways, but almost nothing had changed. It was true that they were thought to be the best pair to go on missions, but they never really spent more than a few minutes together. They were always too busy, having to dash here and there to save lives.

In truth, though they were a pair, they never really had to stay together for too long.

Until today.

Scotti had been the one driving. It didn't happen often, but it did today. And of all days, it was this one that all the seats were occupied, save the one right in front, next to her.

Scotti had frozen right there, sitting behind the wheel. Her hands on the steering tightened so much her veins stood and she had to slow her breathing.

At first, she thought it was the shock of it that made her body react that way. But she realized too quickly that that was only the reaction of a body tied taut to a leash when all she terribly wanted was just in front of her, so close she could reach out and touch her.

Scotti dragged her nearly limp body across the room. These days she wasn't even sure if she was happy to wake anymore. Her body felt restless and tired, as though it needed to be put on hibernation like a big brown bear.

Scotti had found out some weeks ago that Naomi was in therapy. But her mind didn't know what to do with that information so she'd stowed it away in the corner of her mind.

This morning, it seemed to throb from that corner of her mind. Scotti decided to ignore it and get ready for work.

Her captain, in the past weeks, had tried to get information from her about her and Naomi, sensing that something was wrong. Scotti was afraid to paint Naomi in a certain light to the captain. Besides, their team still worked fine, breakup or not, so she told the captain that nothing was different, they were probably only a little busier than before.

It was the captain, who was in therapy too, who had told Scotti that Naomi was in therapy, having seen her leaving the office several times.

Scotti found herself worrying about it this morning. Naomi had once talked about hating therapy and finding it meaningless. So hearing that she was in therapy now bothered Scotti.

Had Naomi developed a drinking issue after they'd broken up? It wasn't very likely considering that Naomi was a doctor who was very invested in making healthy choices for her body.

Scotti worried about how life was going for Naomi. Too many times, she'd considered having a date with Naomi. She'd told herself that it'd be a date with no strings attached. They'd just eat out, go see some cars, and then go home. She told herself it was just to strengthen the work bond between them, just so that their past didn't come between their responsibilities in their respective professions.

But even as the lie rolled off her tongue while she repeated the words to herself in the mirror, she knew that giving herself such hope was cruel. There was no way that could happen and she wouldn't end up in Naomi's bed later that night, holding her to her chest right where it ached now from her absence.

Scotti thought she also needed to be in therapy. She feared that whatever kept her going each morning was going to give up one day and she'd crash against the ground, into her many broken pieces.

Scotti wondered what Naomi felt toward her now—resentment, disappointment or perhaps indifference. Options of better opinions crossed her mind, but Scotti shut them all out, insisting instead to leave hope out of what she felt.

A slight glimpse into Naomi's mind may have

presented itself about a week ago, when on a mission, Scotti had taken off her gloves again.

She hadn't realized that Naomi was standing only a few paces away, at a good distance enough to see Scotti's hands. For the first time since the day they broke up, Naomi saw Scotti's hands.

The burns had healed very quickly, but the scars were there. Scotti had looked up and found Naomi staring. When their eyes met, it'd only been for a second. It was enough time for Scotti to see the death in her eyes, how frigid only a look at it made her. Naomi turned and walked very briskly away from the spot.

Scotti hadn't seen her again until when it was time to go.

Scotti stared now at her scars, wondering if it was really worth it that she'd broken up with Naomi.

So what if Naomi couldn't handle seeing her in pain or wounded? Some people would die to have someone dote over them as Naomi did her.

Again, as Scotti thought this, she reminded herself, *Some people, not me. Not me.*

Scotti sighed deeply as she shrugged her coat on.

She would need some therapy later on if things continued this way.

14

NAOMI

When morning came and Naomi realized that she had fallen asleep at long last, she was relieved. To her surprise, she'd slept longer than she should have and was now behind schedule by about thirty minutes. She still felt exhausted to the bone, but a little sleep was better than none at all.

According to her timetable, she should have a session with Barb later this morning. If she hurried now, there was a chance she'd be able to make it in time. There was a lot she wanted to say to her. They were not new things, but they just needed to get off her chest following the insomnia she had struggled with the night before. However,

Naomi believed she could guess what Barb would say in response; the very things she said almost every time: "Give it time."

For a moment, Naomi pondered about visiting Barb today. At some point the previous night, she had almost called Barb to cry or rant. But that was before she'd chosen to call Scotti instead.

Naomi decided it wasn't worth it, hurrying up just to meet Barb this morning. She chose to miss her appointment this morning. There would be work waiting for her today, hopefully. She'd postponed a number of minor surgeries and hoped at least one of them had landed on today's schedule. She made a mental note to check that as soon as she got to the hospital.

Remembering she'd flung her phone somewhere, Naomi went in search of it. It didn't take her a long while before she found it where it had fallen by the bed. At her touch, it came alive.

She frowned at a missed call from an odd number on her phone.

It could be Scott or Scott's wife.

A second look at the phone made her realize that the call had come in not too long ago.

She still had her phone in her hand when it began to vibrate. She hadn't even looked at it when her mind started to bring up ideas on what response to give Scott following the accidental call from last night.

Then her eyes set on the caller id, and she nearly dropped the phone. She tightened her grip around it as her heart began to thud.

This time, it wasn't Scott but Scotti.

This was a call she'd waited for weeks to receive, but now she did not know how to react to it other than shock. If she missed this opportunity, chances were that she was going to regret it terribly on another night when it was just herself and her thoughts again.

Naomi pressed the pickup button and put the phone to her ear.

"Hello, Scotti?" Naomi greeted.

There was a pause for a moment before she heard Scotti's voice. "Hello Doctor Crane."

Naomi's heart skipped a beat.

Never had she had a problem with being called by her title and last name. But when Scotti said it, there was something amiss about it, in a way that was more about pasts than pronunciation.

Naomi didn't know what to say any after hearing that formal greeting, and she didn't know what to expect, so she was glad that Scotti went straight to the point with what she had to say.

"Don't bother going to the office. There's a fire at St. Mike's. The trucks are on their way there, but the EMS truck will be coming by your street and pick you up in five, if you're ready."

There wasn't much thinking to do. Scotti's call was work-related, and Naomi got focused. "Honk when you're at my place. I'll be ready."

15

SCOTTI

Although they arrived at the scene of the fire as quickly as they could, the fire's damage had already spread. From information gathered, the people had assumed they could put out the fire in the beginning. This had been entirely unsuccessful as the fire had grown rapidly. Most of the people had gotten out but there was an injured person trapped upstairs and the entrance was blocked by the fire.

Scotti set up a stationary hose that would continue to spray water at the door while another firefighter setup the ladder platform that would take some firefighters up the roof where they could fight the fire from above.

They needed Naomi to enter the building and stabilise a casualty. Scotti wasn't at all happy about it, but it was about saving lives and that was what they were both there for.

It was one of things that made Naomi stand out in her medical profession. They had trained Naomi in the use of breathing apparatus and basic firefighting at the fire station. She knew how to maneuver and adjust more than the average emergency medical specialist.

So, not only was she a world class research doctor and cardio-thoracic surgeon, she was also fast becoming an exceptional field medic.

Scotti watched as Naomi donned fire gear and breathing apparatus as though it was something she did every day.

That was the thing about Naomi. She calmly and capably took on any challenge in front of her. Scotti had worked with many doctors in her time and didn't know any others who would happily take on the challenges Naomi had.

"I'll lead Doctor Crane in to the casualty," Scotti offered and her team knew better than to challenge her decision.

Naomi's bright green eyes met hers momentarily as she put her mask on and started breathing through it.

"OK, I'm ready," she nodded.

The ladder platform team got Scotti and Naomi an entrance point in via the attic- it was the most direct route to the casualty. Naomi landed in the cleared attic behind Scotti, her medical kit clanking by her side.

"Come with me!" Scotti told Naomi as soon as she landed behind her. Naomi followed as Scotti carefully navigated a path in the building. It was hard to tell which room they walked into because the fire's soot and smoke had clouded everywhere.

They reached the casualty finally. An unconscious man on the floor in the smoke.

Scotti took to her radio as Naomi began examining and working on the man.

"We are with the casualty. White male. 50s. Unconscious. He is trapped under some metalwork."

"His breathing is shallow." Naomi pointed out to her. "He won't make it out alive without treatment. It looks like a hemothorax. I'm going to need insert a chest tube between his ribs to drain it which will hopefully stabilise him and then you can cut him free. Ok?"

Scotti nodded. "Got it." Scotti watched Naomi work with the scalpel cutting through his skin and intercostal muscles and then inserting a tube. She was calm and confident in her work and it was a beautiful thing to watch.

Oh how she wished everything had ended differently. Or more accurately, not ended at all.

"Doctor Crane is inserting a chest tube to stabilise the patient and then I am going to cut him free." Scotti radioed back to the Captain.

"OK, great. Pulse has improved, breathing is much better. He is stable. Go for it with your cutting." Naomi rocked back onto her heels and gestured for Scotti to get involved.

Scotti already had her tools ready and wasted no time in cutting him free.

They strapped him to the spinal board they had brought in with them ready to get him moved. It was all going so smoothly. The smoke was clearing greatly.

Scotti smiled at Naomi and Naomi met her with a smile more genuine than anything Scotti had seen from her since the break up. Even though a mask, Scotti could see the light in her eyes.

"We make a good team." Naomi said. "Well done. That was impressive." Was Scotti imagining things or was Naomi looking almost flirtatious behind her mask.

"You are the impressive one. You are so smooth and so skilled in your work. It is an honor to watch you. This guy is lucky to have you in his corner today."

"Let's go." Naomi said and they lifted the stretcher.

Scotti had a fleeting thought that she should recheck the integrity of the floor on their path back, but she decided to do it as they went.

Just as they were nearly back to the ladder platform, Naomi stepped slightly off path and the floor immediately collapsed under her.

"Naomi!!!!" Scotti felt the scream coming from her mouth as she reacted immediately leaping to try and save Naomi, but there was no saving her.

Naomi fell, the man on the stretcher fell and Scotti fell too.

Scotti felt herself hit the ground on the floor below and crumple in a heap.

"FUCK!" she shouted. This was the last thing she needed. Certainly the last thing the guy on the stretcher needed. Most importantly where was Naomi? Was Naomi ok?

"Naomi?" Scotti called as she sat up and looked around.

"Ugh. I'm ok, I think. Just bruised." Naomi's voice responded quickly and Scotti moved towards it in the smoke. She felt something- it was Naomi. Great. It felt better to be close to her. It also felt much hotter down here and Scotti knew that was never a good thing.

They also didn't have a hose reel with them and that also was a really bad thing.

Scotti screwed up her face in the dark. This was not a good situation. How was she going to get them out of it?

"The guy... where is the guy?" Naomi murmured and it sounded like she was searching from him. Scotti pulled out her infra red camera as she knew that her flash light would be no use. They weren't in normal darkness, this was thick black smoke, she could feel it.

Her camera came to life and immediately showed her the location of the man on the stretcher.

Unfortunately it also showed her the extent of the fire surrounding them. Sometimes smoke is so thick that you don't see the flames and Scotti knew well that was about as serious as any situation she could imagine.

She pulled the emergency tag on her breathing apparatus. When she pulled this tag it emitted an eerie wailing sound. It was only to be pulled in the most dire situation possible. It made every other firefighter know that a firefighter was in lethal danger.

She pulled Naomi's tag too.

"SOS Firefighter Saunders. Doctor Crane. Male casualty. SOS We fell through the floor. Surrounded by fire. No firefighting media present." Scotti relayed the situation through her radio. Meanwhile she reached the man on the stretcher and did what she could to put a spare mask on him and tried to cover him with a fireproof blanket. She didn't rate his chances.

Fuck, this is bad. This is really bad. The casualty will die. I will die and Naomi will die too.

In her fear, she hardly realized when she took Naomi's hand in hers and squeezed it.

"There's a lot of fire in here, Naomi."

There were tears welling up in her eyes and her voice was breaking.

"I don't know how to get us out."

There was no way out of here and she knew it.

Naomi was quiet and squeezed her hand right back.

"They could come and save us though, right?

Scotti nodded slowly although she knew Naomi couldn't see her. She knew it was unlikely now. She knew they had barely any time and as she looked at the gauge on her breathing apparatus it only added to the feeling of impending doom within her. "They could," she whispered.

There's no time!!!

She needed Naomi. If she was going to die, she didn't want to do it denying the life she always wanted. Her senses felt overloaded and her eyes shut as she squeezed Naomi's hand once again, perhaps for the last time.

"I love you. I haven't stopped loving you. I can't help but love you. I don't have all the words, but I need to let you know that if there's a next life and a chance with you, I'd run for it with all that I am." Scotti could hear the pain and the tears in her own voice.

Then, Naomi spoke, "I got into therapy because I wanted to have a second opportunity with you. I didn't want to stop all that you can be. I didn't want my fears to be the reason you don't live your fullest. That's not what love is. Love ought to push you beyond limits and hold your hand when you fall. I wasn't doing that, but I want to be that for you, Scotti. So it hurt me each time I checked and I wasn't good enough to come back to you. It's you I've always wanted, Scotti. It's you who pushes me to be better. I look at you saving lives; I look at the way you devote yourself to fire and rescue and I'm in awe of how incredible you are. If there's a life that I can get a second chance with you, Scotti, you won't have to find me. I'll be right there with you. I love you, Scotti."

Scotti felt her heart leap. Naomi loved her after all. She held Naomi tightly to her and Naomi leaned into her.

She checked her air gauge again and she checked Naomi's.

The eery wailing of their emergency sirens continued in the background alongside the crackling of the flames which just got louder and louder.

Just as she had gotten everything she ever wanted, she was going to lose it all.

"Mayday! Mayday!" Scotti called into her radio. "Please, come in... someone... anyone..."

16

NAOMI

Naomi felt like she was floating in another world. Was she dead?

"Doctor Crane..."

"Naomi..."

Naomi opened her eyes to see the hospital. She could recognise a hospital room when she saw one.

She narrowed her eyes. She was in the ER. She was on a bed. She must have made it out of the fire somehow. She was alive. Thank god.

She panicked and sat bolt upright. She saw Dr. Cora Hope and Dr. Agnes Frame. She was grateful to be with them and alive, but there was only one person she needed to see right now. "Scotti! Where is she? Is she ok?"

Cora stood aside and behind her, just coming slowly through the doorway to her room wearing her red fire department T shirt that had just about survived their ordeal was Scotti.

Naomi would have jumped out of the bed but she realised she was attached to an oxygen mask. She pulled it off her.

Tears streamed from her eyes as she sat on the edge of the bed holding Scotti's face in her hands and kissing her repeatedly all over.

"Oh.. Scotti... I love you..."

In between kisses the words poured out that she had been dying to say all along and she meant them now with every fiber of her being. She could smell that beautifully familiar sweet smokiness of Scotti

"I'm so sorry..."

"Are you ok?"

"I'll support you always, you know..."

"I want you to do what you love..."

"I can never ever be without you again..."

She felt Scotti's strong hands on her shoulders, pulling her back. She never wanted to let go of

Scotti. Never wanted to stop kissing her. But she let Scotti pull her back.

"I love you, too." Scotti smiled at her. Battered, bruised, dirty, bloodied, beautiful Scotti.

"How did we get out?" Naomi asked.

"Your air ran out. I knew you would be dead within a minute if I didn't do something drastic. I dragged you through the fire and broke down a wall. Luckily the wall was compromised anyway and my team was on the other side. They saved us."

"You saved me, Scotti. Again. You are a hero and I can't believe I ever wanted you to stop. Of course, I'm scared of losing you. But I've learnt to understand that fear and process my feelings over losing Sasha."

Naomi sighed deeply. Why had it taken them almost dying for everything to become so clear?

"I promise things will be different now, Scotti. I promise I will give you all the love and support you deserve. If you can forgive me, please let me spend the rest of my life making it up to you."

Scotti took Naomi's hands in her own strong hands. Naomi felt the scars on her palms, but it didn't scare her now. She suddenly knew that everyone's time is limited and that when it is your time to go, it is your time to go. She knew for sure she needed to spend every moment possible with Scotti for as long as they both had on this earth.

Scotti's kind navy blue eyes fixed hers. Scotti looked like she had just left a war zone, but Naomi thought she had never been more lovely. Scotti was the purest most lovely soul on the planet, surely.

"You are the most incredible woman I have ever met. I can't wait to spend the rest of forever with you," she smiled and she leant in and kissed Naomi tenderly.

Naomi felt the world around her swimming. She had been drowning and Scotti was her air.

She lost herself in the kiss.

The kiss that saved her.

The kiss that healed her.

The kiss that was the beginning of their future together.

"I love you so much," she whispered against Scotti's lips.

EPILOGUE

The hallway was full of people. Scotti had long lost count of how many of them she could recognize.

She raised her head above the people, her eyes searching for just one person. When she didn't find her, she put down the glass of wine she had in her hands, excused herself from the rest of the circle, and disappeared behind one of the rooms.

Her cheeks hurt from beaming all morning. Naomi's speech had made her cry.

It was Naomi who she was looking for in the crowd of people.

It was their day, truly, but Scotti had been looking for a moment to steal Naomi to herself.

"Scotti!" Someone grabbed her arm. She turned to find Cora.

"Jesus, Cora! I'm so glad you're here. Damn! You found the time!" Scotti greeted excitedly.

"Miss this? Me? Never. Congratulations, Scotti. You guys are such a wonderful sight for everyone's eyes."

Scotti put her hand on her heart and pouted her lips. "Thank you, Cora. Has Naomi seen you around? She'd squeal."

"Oh," Cora waved modestly, "That's part of what I'm here for."

Cora was Naomi's consultant on Naomi's most recent scientific breakthrough. After the research facility had burned down, Naomi had worked with the other departments. It had taken about two years to rebuild but once it was rebuilt, Naomi had restarted her research.

The press conference for it had been held just the week before and it had gathered a lot of attention from everywhere in the world.

This event was an after-party following the achievement. Scotti had been the one to plan it all as a surprise and present for their wedding anniversary.

She'd only told Naomi about it a few days ago

when she had taken her out to shop for their outfits.

Together, they had sent out invites to everyone who knew them. However, Scotti hadn't expected this kind of a crowd, though she had prepared for it.

All morning, so many people had walked up to her and Naomi with gifts and hugs and thanked them for saving their lives.

It made Scotti emotional that she'd been able to do so much for so many people. Even more, it made her more excited about Naomi's research project. It was designed to save more people than they ever would have thought possible. The work had yet to be materialized but it had gotten past the paperwork stage and the production was already underway.

There were still more people downstairs, but right there on the staircase, Scotti's eyes fell on Naomi and distinguished her from the crowd.

Her incredible wife was always stunning but tonight, especially so in a blood red cocktail dress; a long straight sleeveless gown with a thigh high slit that made Scotti's fingers curious to disappear into it. She loved the way the dress hugged Naomi's hips and curves. Naomi's nude heels were the perfect pick for the dress. Later, they'd take a lot of pictures.

As though she suspected she was being watched, Naomi turned around and her eyes immediately found Scotti.

The unspoken bond they had between them was second to none. After everything they had been through, they wanted to make the most of every minute.

Excusing herself from her circle of friends, she detached herself from the group and began to ascend the flight of stairs.

"Hey, I've been looking all over for you," Scotti said as Naomi met her lips with hers. Their kiss was electric but also felt like coming home. However that balance worked.

"I've been attending to the guests. Damn, there are so many of them, have we really saved this many lives? Are people just pretending?" Naomi joked.

It was nearly unbelievable for her, considering that not all the people were there in person, yet had called in ahead of the day and sent in presents.

This moment was a dream come true; a dream

she would have thoroughly denied four years ago when she thought they were going to die.

But now they were two years into marriage and still felt the same for each other as they had since the very beginning.

"Damn, Scotti, I don't know how you pulled this off, especially under my nose all the while."

"Oh, please, busy bee. It's not that hard."

Naomi laughed. Her hands went around Scotti's neck. They were vaguely aware of the fact that they were still there on the steps and nearly everyone could see them. To them, it was just themselves they could see.

"I saw your former captain somewhere around," Naomi mentioned.

"Really?" Scotti's eyes widened.

After the incident where they were trapped by the fire, Scotti realized that news of her bravado had spread. She had saved the famous Doctor Naomi Crane. Again. The press visited and interviewed, and the news carried the story. She felt a bit of a fraud for this one, as if it hadn't been for her team on the other side of that crumbling wall seeking out the wailing sirens that signalled 'Firefighter down' neither of them would have survived. Her decision to move Naomi and try and get through a wall had been luck rather than judgement. It was Naomi. Brave, beautiful, super smart, Naomi. The love of her life. She couldn't have just sat by surrounded by flames and let her die when her air ran out. Nevertheless, she figured she had done enough actual hero stuff in the past to perhaps warrant the attention. Not long after, she was promoted to captain.

Being captain meant having an even more hectic schedule and more responsibility. But Scotti loved that and had never failed in her duties. Being Captain meant she went into fires a lot less often and although the old Scotti would have always said that wasn't what she wanted, the new Scotti definitely had a peace with it.

A small blonde girl toddled towards her and reached up her arms. "Mama,"

Scotti beamed with love and pride. If there was one person on this planet she loved as much as she loved Naomi, it was Romily. "Hey baby girl." She scooped her up and kissed her all over her face until she was giggling.

Scotti had never been afraid of dying. But, she was afraid of losing Naomi and Romily. And dying would mean losing Naomi and Romily, losing her greatest loves.

Ashley the nanny showed up. "Do you want me to take Romily for a bit, give you guys some time."

"That would be great, thanks Ashley."

"I think I saw Agnes somewhere too. She was probably the first person here this morning."

"Yeah, she's in the back. There are people in the swimming pool."

"There are people everywhere," Naomi said.

Scotti gave her a naughty look. "I know somewhere where there are no people," she said.

"Trust me, Scotti, there are people in the bathroom too."

Scotti grabbed Naomi's hand. "You've been so hardworking, Naomi. You deserve to see how many lives you've touched. I've been meaning to say that to you all morning."

Naomi's eyes glistened, thoroughly touched.

"But I have a little something for you, for all the hard work."

Naomi narrowed her eyes and arched her brow. "Is it what I think it is?" They were walking now, waving at people as they passed. Soft music played in the background as their guests danced and sang.

Naomi wondered what Scotti was up to. Scotti

had already given her a lot for one day and she was unable to guess what was coming now.

Until they stopped in front of their bedroom and Scotti opened the door to let her in.

"I'm sure our guests won't mind if we're gone for just a few minutes," Scotti said, her voice becoming naughty.

She shrugged her jacket off, at the same time, unbuttoning her pants.

Naomi took off her heels and peeled her clothes off her body. She'd been waiting for this moment all day.

They collided before they had all their clothes off. Scotti kissed Naomi hard and fast and let her take her pants off.

Now it was just the two of them in their underwear.

"Did I tell you?" Naomi said, starting to giggle as Scotti's curious fingers shifted her panties, and began to push inside her. "I booked us a weekend getaway."

"You're joking? How could you tell I needed that?" Scotti inserted a third finger and Naomi moaned. The sound reverberated on Scotti's inside and she stroked Naomi's clitoris faster with her thumb. Naomi swore. Scotti's free hand found

Naomi's nipple as they stumbled back onto the bed. When Scotti's wet tongue rolled over her breasts, Naomi's eyes rolled back into her head, and she groaned.

Scotti laughed, shushing her. "You don't want our guests to know we're having the best time without them."

Naomi sat up and pushed Scotti back gently by her shoulders until it was Scotti whose back was now on the bed. Scotti liked the way Naomi's breasts bounced whenever she moved while she was naked. It made her wet. But she wasn't satisfied with touching Naomi.

When Naomi sat on her face, Scotti groaned happily. She ran her tongue over Naomi's vulva, making her squirm and squeal. She sucked at Naomi's clitoris while Naomi 's hands tangled in her hair.

Scotti sucked and bit Naomi's clitoris softly. There was hardly a break between Naomi's moans and gasps.

When she finally ejaculated, it was all over Scotti's tongue, filling her mouth and spilling out over her chin.

Fuck, she is so incredible.

Scotti could never quite believe how insatiable

her appetite still was for her wife. It was one thing that had never waned. Naomi's desire had been less in the first year or so after having Romily, but it was back now. Back with a vengeance and Scotti was here for it.

"Get on top of me," Naomi whispered to Scotti as soon as she had stopped shaking. Scotti was already very wet and near her own orgasm. But Naomi wasn't going to let her off that easily.

As she stripped her underwear off and straddled Naomi's hips, she began to grind and it felt exquisite. She stopped grinding to allow Naomi's burrowing fingers to enter her and she relished every second of them pushing inside her. She sat back down so she could grind her clitoris against whatever she could at the same time as feeling Naomi's fingers pulling her open. She could feel them against her G spot. She felt Naomi pushing another finger inside her and another. She wanted it all and more. Scotti knew she would beg for anything Naomi had to give her, it was though she had no limits with Naomi.

She felt herself in a daze. It had been a while since they had fucked, between work and caring for Romily, their opportunities to lose themselves in each other weren't quite as often as they used to be.

"Please.. uh... more.." Scotti growled. She was sitting upright now, still straddling Naomi's hips. She knew what she was asking of Naomi and Naomi knew too and Scotti wiggled her hips and adjusted to allow Naomi the angle she needed. Scotti was so very wet, although Naomi withdrew her fingers and added saliva, Scotti knew that Naomi's whole hand would soon slide inside of her and she couldn't wait.

Naomi tucked her fingers together into a duck beak shape and began to push back inside of Scotti. Scotti adjusted to help her. Her knuckles caught a bit, it was the widest point. Scotti knew this and bore down on Naomi's hand. She wanted to take Naomi's fist so very badly. It was one of her absolute favorite things.

She felt Naomi's whole hand slide inside of her and she lost herself in the moment. She felt herself moaning loudly and grinding down. She thought she felt Naomi's other hand against her clitoris and her orgasm took over her entire body as it crashed through her.

Naomi took Scotti's body to places she had never been.

Fuck, that was incredible.

When Naomi's hand finally slid out of her, Scotti collapsed down onto the bed and laid beside her, and they held each other right there for many minutes.

It was Saturday morning when their bodies seemed to have recovered from all the activities they did all week long. By then they were in their bed in the hotel room Naomi had gotten reservations for.

Naomi was awake before Scotti was. She didn't wake her, knowing they had a busy day ahead of them. She sat in bed, stroking Scotti's short blonde hair, reflecting on the past week.

She'd been blown away when Scotti told her that she'd organized a party on their anniversary.

That surprise had nearly matched the surprise she'd given Scotti when Naomi had gotten down on one knee and proposed to Scotti. It was one evening after they had finished a mission and were getting ready to go home for the evening. Right there in Scotti's office, Naomi had asked Scotti to marry her. She was one month out of therapy then and thought that if she didn't show Scotti how serious she was about her at that moment, she was once again going to have to wait for Scotti to make the move.

When Scotti had cried and said yes, Naomi's joy had known no bounds.

Somehow, even all this time later, it still felt like a dream. It felt unreal that, somehow, she'd gotten out of therapy healed enough to decide that Scotti was the one for her no matter what.

It wasn't that she'd gotten over her fear of Scotti getting hurt, it was that it didn't limit her anymore. Scotti still could get hurt on the job; Naomi still got scared. But she understood that it was because she loved Scotti that she didn't want her to get hurt. So whenever Scotti came home hurt, Naomi was the first one there, reassuring Scotti regardless of her own fears.

Naomi was Scotti's biggest support in her profession.

Having a baby with Scotti was everything Naomi wanted to make their family complete. She hadn't ever thought it was something she would do, and at her age, she hadn't really known it would be possible. But, it had been possible. She had gotten pregnant quickly and Romily was the greatest gift she could imagine. Seeing how great Scotti was with Romily just made her heart feel so full.

Overwhelmed now, Naomi kissed Scotti's forehead. Scotti stirred and Naomi watched her wake.

Later that morning, they were taking a walk through the extensive gardens when Naomi pulled Scotti into herself and whispered, "I love you, Scotti. I love everything that you are, that you embody, that you do, that you think of, that you decide. I love you, Captain Scotti."

Scotti looked at her lovingly. "You make my *I love you* sound basic. But I hope this kiss passes the message at least a little."

Scotti kissed Naomi with all the passion there was in the world.

FREE BOOK

I really hope you enjoyed this story. I loved writing it.

I'd love for you to get my FREE book- Her Boss- by joining my mailing list. Just click on the following link or type into your web browser: https://BookHip.com/MNVVPBP

Meg has had a huge crush on her hot older boss for some time now. Could it be possible that her crush is reciprocated? https://BookHip.com/MNVVPBP

ALSO BY EMILY HAYES

If you liked this story, I think you will love the next one-
Hearts Clash!

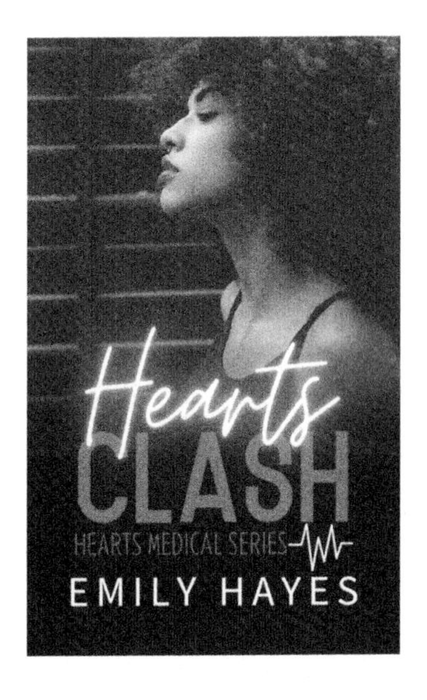

She finds a genuine connection online. What will she do when she finds out who her new crush really is?

mybook.to/Hearts4

Printed in Great Britain
by Amazon

43267545R00129